Lesbian SEX Chronicles

FIRST SESSION

TOI MCMULLEN

Toi Box Publishing
Houston, TX

LESBIAN SEX CHRONICLES: FIRST SESSION
This book is a work of fiction. Names, characters, places, and incidents are the product of the author's imagination or are used fictitiously. Any resemblance to actual events, locales, or persons, living or dead, is strictly coincidental.

LESBIAN SEX CHRONICLES:
FIRST SESSION © 2020 Latauria McMullen

ISBN: 978-0-578-68883-1

Published by Toi Box Publishing
Houston, TX

Printed in the United States of America
First Edition June 2019

Cover Design by: Make Your Mark Publishing Solutions
Interior Layout by: Make Your Mark Publishing Solutions
Editing: Make Your Mark Publishing Solutions
Book Cover Photo: Erica Jones, Instagram:
@quantum_black_photography

CONTENTS

ACKNOWLEDGEMENTS

To the woman who taught me how to properly masturbate, thanks! Seriously, though—before you came along, I didn't know what the hell I was doing. Sad to say, but I had it all wrong. I can happily say I'm a pro at it now. Aside from that, you were the first person I felt comfortable expressing my fears and truths to. I appreciate the happiness we shared together.

To the other women who have shared a bed with me, I was able to learn something from each of you, so thanks for the experience.

To my personal self-publishing assistant, Monique D. Mensah with Make Your Mark Publishing Solutions, I'm so happy you slid into my DMs on Instagram! I was searching for a self-publishing company when I wrote my first novel and didn't have any luck. I ended up doing everything by myself and was so stressed out. Once I went to your page, I had to hit the follow button. Tuesday Tea is one of my faves. I apologize again for changing the starting date twice. Thank you for being patient with me.

DEDICATION

To my life partner, Nicole. Sometimes I'm all over the place and can be a bit much, but here you are, soaking it all in. I'm not sure how you deal with me and my jumbled thoughts, but thank you for loving all the parts of me that even I can't understand. I know you love me exactly as I am, and that alone makes my heart smile. I want you to know that you inspire me, even though you feel like you're not creative. I love you, and you're absolutely amazing.

Xoxo

Photographer: SMI Photography

AUTHOR'S NOTE

How do lesbians have sex? I've been asked that question one too many times. Straight people don't realize how rude that question is. It's like lesbians are an endangered species to be marveled at. We have sex like heterosexuals... with a few unfamiliar techniques that a straight person might want to know.

Penetration isn't the only way a woman can reach an orgasm, but some assume that it is. Stimulation is a marvelous wonder. I can't say I know everything, but I know quite a bit. Have you ever heard the saying, "Two pussies can't bump?" I'm laughing as I type that because I particularly love grinding my pussy up against my girlfriend's. The feeling is so sumptuous! I look forward to having a woman in between my legs. The general rule to pussy grinding is finding an angle that is mutually pleasurable. Once you find it, you'll feel like you're in heaven.

Aside from pussy grinding, there's always a good tongue fucking. Women eat pussy better than men; that's not up for debate with me. I've walked the straight line, and there's a difference in the tongue stroke. Actually, I just lied, I've never been straight. I found women attractive long before my first sexual experience with a woman. I talked a little about that in my first novel, *Miami Lust*, but let me get back on topic. When it comes to eating pussy, the clit should get most of the attention. If she's not moaning, that's a sure sign you're not doing a good job. I like to use my tongue and fingers.

So that brings us to finger fucking. I feel as though I've mastered it. I like using my thumb or my middle finger. I can use two fingers, but a woman I dated taught me how to satisfy with only one. Thanks for that.

When it comes to sex toys, you can try to figure them out on your own, but it's more fun when you use them with (on) someone else. I didn't really care for them until I got involved with a woman who had an assortment. She hosted passion parties, and she knew exactly what she was doing. She used a wand on me and I damn near lost my mind! The amount of pleasure was so overwhelming, I was in tears.

I've seen plenty of memes and have heard many men say that lesbians shouldn't have the right to use dildos. We can have both worlds if we want to. I've been fucked with a strap-on and have also fucked a woman with a strap. I didn't understand how a woman could reach sexual satisfaction from just wearing one until I experienced it myself. It's so invigorating. It all goes back to stimulation.

I really could go on and on, but it's time for me to switch to narrator mode and get into these characters' stories. The women you are going to read about are fictional characters.

Some of the stories come from my personal life, and some sprang from my imagination. This first session has mild sex stories. The second session will be spicy, so stay tuned.

I also want to say thanks for taking the time to venture into my mind. I hope you enjoy reading this as much as I've enjoyed writing it.

TRINITY

One in a Million

The rain continued to pour down as Trinity traveled home. She wasn't sure why, but whenever it rained, she would get extra horny. Something about the sound of the water thumping against the car made her pussy throb uncontrollably. She literally had chills running through her body and she desperately needed some pleasure to help calm her hormones down. She felt like she could explode at any moment. Aside from the rain, it had been four days since she had seen Tiffany, her girlfriend. The anticipation was damn near killing her.

The drive to the home they shared was only twenty minutes from the airport, but it felt as if it was taking her forever to get there. The radio wasn't helping her situation either, because nothing but sensual love songs from the 90s kept playing.

She smiled when Aaliyah's song, "One in a Million," came on. That song depicted exactly how she felt about Tiffany. Tiffany was the light on her dark days, and she was more than grateful for her. They connected spiritually, emotionally and mentally. She could tell Tiffany anything, and vice versa. She was the true definition of a friend and a lover. Trinity didn't believe there was such a thing as a soulmate until Tiffany swept her off her feet. It was a little sticky and messy, but they connected right away. Trinity was as clumsy as they come. She was always wasting something or tripping over something.

The day she and Tiffany met, Trinity had bought a caramel macchiato and had her head down while she was walking and staring at her cell phone. She didn't see Tiffany until it was too late; she ran right into her and dropped her cup on the floor. The top flew off when it hit the ground and some of the hot liquid splashed onto Tiffany's pants and shoes.

"Oh no! I am so sorry! I should have been paying attention to where I was going. I'll clean that up for you!" Trinity exclaimed, rushing to grab some napkins. Trinity would have been pissed off if something like that had happened to her, so she felt really bad about it. Tiffany seemed calm about the situation, as if it was something that happened to her on a regular basis.

"It's alright," Tiffany laughed. "It's my fault for wearing white jeans to a coffee shop. Tell you what: I'll buy you another one as long as you promise not to waste it on me."

Trinity laughed nervously. That wasn't the response she was expecting, and she hadn't made eye contact with Tiffany until that exact moment. She liked what she saw, so it was hard for her not to blush. Tiffany's almond-shaped eyes seemed to sparkle. She had a distinctive broad nose and a full mouth. Her sand-colored skin looked so soft, Trinity wanted to reach out and rub her hand across Tiffany's face. Her oval-shaped head was so cute. One side was shaved, and her faux locs were pulled into a ponytail. She was dressed in a masculine style, but her beauty really shined through. Tiffany was much taller than Trinity, and that was a first. Trinity was taller than every woman she had dated, so she wasn't used to looking up. She looked away once she sensed she had been staring at Tiffany for too long.

Trinity fumbled her fingers nervously. "Um, you really don't have to buy me another one, seeing how it was my fault in the first place. I'll even pay to get your jeans dry-cleaned. Would you like to exchange numbers so I can take care of that for you?"

Tiffany didn't give a verbal response right away; she smiled instead. If Trinity had been two shades lighter, Tiffany would have been able to tell she was blushing. "Do you have some free time on your hands right now?" Tiffany asked, disregarding everything Trinity had said.

Trinity was supposed to meet up with her best friend and her best friend's girlfriend, but she didn't feel like being a third wheel anyway. She told Tiffany she was free. They sat in the coffee shop and talked for hours. It was comforting how they meshed with each other so well. Before they parted, Tiffany asked her out on an official date.

It only took one date for them to start spending all their

free time together. Trinity was the spontaneous one in the relationship, while Tiffany was more calculated. The first year they were together, they didn't have oral sex or use any sex toys. That wasn't Trinity's choice, though; she tried to eat Tiffany's pussy every chance she got, to no avail. Tiffany never told her why she didn't want it, but the first time she allowed Trinity to go down on her, Tiffany stopped her soon after she started. Trinity had never had a woman stop her in the middle of performing.

"Here, let me show you how it's done," she said while rubbing Trinity's arms. She had her lie down on her back and spread her legs open. Once she put her tongue up against Trinity's clit and started slowly moving it up and down, Trinity shook uncontrollably. She was damn near in tears in a matter of minutes. Tiffany gave her the best orgasm she had ever experienced. She'd had a few girlfriends before Tiffany, but none of them matched up with her as well as she did.

"Oh crap!" Trinity yelled. She had been so lost in the memory that she almost passed her house. She pulled into the driveway, parked and flipped down the visor mirror so she could see if she looked as tired as she felt. After being away from Tiffany for so long, she didn't want to come home looking drained. Her glasses were hiding the bags under her eyes, so Trinity was thankful for that. Before she started wearing glasses, people would often tell her that she resembled supermodel Tyra Banks, but she didn't see it, unless they meant she had the same big forehead.

"Ugh! My forehead looks so damn shiny," Trinity said and shook her head disapprovingly. She grabbed at the scrunchie that was barely holding her hair in place and pulled it off. She was glad she had wrapped her hair the night before or else it would have been a tangled mess. She combed through it with her fingers and swooped some over her forehead. "Much better." Trinity smiled with satisfaction as she stepped out of her car. She was sure Tiffany was as anxious as she was to wrap her arms around her.

When Trinity stepped inside her home, her eyes widened and she gasped, raising her hands to her chest. She couldn't believe the beautiful surprise that was in front of her. There was a trail of rose petals that seemingly went on forever from the front door, leading down the hallway toward the bedroom. She closed the door behind her slowly and smiled at the display of burning tea light candles. Tiffany really knew how to make her heart smile. After admiring the scene for a few lingering moments, Trinity made her way to the rest of the surprise. Her heart was racing. She inhaled deeply before turning the door handle and entering the bedroom. Tiffany was lying on her back across their bed with a smile as beautiful as the ambiance. The top to the black silk pajama set she was wearing wasn't completely buttoned, so her breasts were partially exposed. Trinity couldn't help but smile at the sight of her beautiful girlfriend. Tiffany met her gaze and rose slowly from the bed. She grabbed a single rose from the nightstand and made her way to her lover.

"Hello, beautiful," she greeted seductively. "It's been a boring four days without you."

"Tell me about it. I thought about you the whole time… and on the way home. Couldn't wait to get here."

Tiffany smiled. "I'm sure you want to take a shower and relax, but how about I run you a bubble bath?" she cooed, kissing her lover on the lips, "and I can bathe you. How would you like that?"

Trinity smiled. "You're so good to me. I love you."

"I love you more," Tiffany replied and kissed Trinity gently on the lips.

They embraced for a few seconds, and then Tiffany grabbed Trinity's hand and escorted her to the bathroom. There were rose petals in the bathtub and scattered on the floor.

Tiffany sat on the side of the tub and turned on the water. She added A Thousand Wishes to the bath water, but Tiffany only had one wish—to spend the rest of her life with Trinity. She knew Trinity felt the same, so she planned to make this night all about her. While the water was running, Trinity stood back and admired her girlfriend. They had been together for over two years, but their relationship still felt fresh and new.

"What are you smiling about?" Tiffany asked, breaking Trinity out of her thoughts. She was wearing a smile herself.

"I'm smiling at you. You're so thoughtful." She extended her hand and Tiffany kissed it. Trinity blushed.

Tiffany turned the water off and stood up so she could

direct all her attention to Trinity. She removed Trinity's glasses carefully, set them on the sink and then proceeded to undress her. The heat between them rose, and their breathing got faster. The throbbing Trinity felt earlier was back. She wanted Tiffany so badly. If she'd had it her way, they'd already be doing nasty things to each other, but she was going to be patient because the last thing she wanted was to interfere with the mood that Tiffany had set. There would be plenty of time to get down to the business of licking, sucking, and devouring her.

When Trinity slid down into their garden bathtub and Tiffany began to wash her back, she closed her eyes and allowed the softness of Tiffany's touch to soothe her.

"Ah, baby, this feels so good," she said in a low moan. "I've been so tense the past couple of days. My body is thankful for the extra attention." She opened her eyes and smiled again.

"I'm glad I could help you out," Tiffany replied, leaning over and planting a kiss on Trinity's lips.

"Hmm," Trinity moaned. She was ready to feel Tiffany's lips all over her body. Their love-making was electric, to say the least. Each and every time they had sex, it was explosive. Tiffany could make her come with only one finger, but two fingers had her running away and damn near crawling up the walls. Trinity didn't realize fingers could feel so good before she met Tiffany.

"Baby, you know you got me horny, right?" Trinity asked in an enticing tone.

"That was the plan," Tiffany said with a smirk. "Now that I've washed every inch of your body, it's time for your full-body massage," she told Trinity, taking her by the hand and helping her climb out of the tub.

Tiffany dried Trinity off and led her back to their bed. "Lie down on your stomach."

Trinity excitedly did as she was told. Her heart was racing. She had never had a girlfriend bathe her and give her a massage. She took a deep breath and let it out. Tiffany grabbed a bottle of avocado oil from the dresser and drizzled it onto Trinity's umber body. She started massaging Trinity's shoulders and then her back. After that, she drizzled oil on her butt and rubbed it in. Trinity took another deep breath and then exhaled. She was in heaven.

"I want you to turn over," Tiffany whispered in her ear. Trinity obliged and rolled over to her back. The way Tiffany was staring into her eyes sent chills up and down Trinity's spine. She saw love and admiration staring back at her, and it filled her with so much joy. Tiffany kissed her on the forehead and poured more oil into her hands. She started massaging Trinity's shoulders slowly and moved down to her breasts. Trinity shuddered when Tiffany started massaging the inside of her thighs.

"Oh! Baby, this feels so good," she cooed.

Tiffany didn't reply; she only continued to massage. She had Trinity turn back onto her stomach so she could pour some oil on her. She applied the right amount of pressure as she continued to massage Trinity's body.

"You know, I've never done this before," Tiffany mentioned as she was massaging Trinity's lower back.

"Really? I can't tell. It seems like you're a professional masseuse," Trinity replied in a voice barely above a whisper. She couldn't recall a time when she had felt so relaxed. Tiffany's hands were working their magic all over her body. But then, Tiffany stopped.

Trinity could feel Tiffany's breath on her ear as she whispered, "I want you to sit on my face."

Chills ran up and down Trinity's spine again. They adjusted their bodies so Tiffany could lie on her back. Trinity straddled Tiffany's head. Tiffany slid her tongue across Trinity's clit very slowly. Trinity shuddered again and squealed with delight. She started gyrating on Tiffany's tongue. The pleasure was so intense and overpowering, she had tears streaming down her face. Tiffany gripped her wrists.

"Yes! Oh, baby! I love you so much!" Trinity cried out. Her body was trembling, but Tiffany didn't stop licking and sucking until she had her fill. Trinity climaxed then collapsed on top of Tiffany. She had reached her sexual peak and could barely move. She smiled weakly at her.

"I love you, too," Tiffany told her after she kissed Trinity on the forehead.

Trinity didn't realize she had drifted off to sleep until she woke up to the aroma of food cooking. She smiled; she had planned on taking Tiffany out to breakfast, but she was fine with them staying in and enjoying each other's company. She grabbed her glasses off the nightstand, slid out of bed and stepped into her unicorn slippers. Her hair was all over the place, but she didn't mind. She walked into the kitchen and saw Tiffany in a sports bra and basketball shorts, standing in front of the stove, cooking. Trinity eased up behind Tiffany and wrapped her arms around Tiffany's waist.

"Morning, sleepy head," Tiffany said as she placed her hands on top of Trinity's. "Have a seat. The food is almost done." Trinity kissed her on the cheek and did as she was instructed. A few minutes later, Tiffany put a plate down in front of her. "You can start eating without me. I have something for you I need to go grab."

Trinity's face lit up like a child's on Christmas morning. She couldn't believe she was getting another surprise.

"Ooh! What is it?" she squealed with excitement.

Tiffany didn't answer; she only smiled and left the room. Trinity was so anxious to see what Tiffany would return with, she didn't even want to touch her omelet. She really wanted to get up and take a peek around the corner, but she didn't want to ruin Tiffany's surprise. Trinity stood up when she heard music playing but didn't leave the table. She knew what song it was as soon as the beat dropped.

Dru Hill, "Beauty"—it was one of Trinity's all-time favorite songs. The current R&B music on the radio was nothing compared to the tunes of the 90s. The song continued to play, but Tiffany still had not appeared. Trinity stepped away from the table and went to the refrigerator to get something to drink.

When she turned around to sit back down, Tiffany was back in the kitchen and down on one knee. She was holding a small black box. It wasn't open, but Trinity knew exactly what was inside. Her heart fluttered, and for a second, she thought she was about to faint. "Ba-by," she was barely able to stammer out.

"Trinity Jade Rice, will you marry me?" Tiffany asked, trying to open the box with a shaky hand. Even though she believed Trinity would say yes, Tiffany was still nervous. It felt like it was taking forever for Trinity to give her an answer, even though not even a second had passed.

Trinity could barely open her mouth. Tears of joy were flowing down her face. This was the happiest moment in her life. "Of course, I'll marry you!" she exclaimed, jumping up and down.

Tiffany finally got the box open and took out the ring. She slid it gently onto Trinity's ring finger. Trinity took a good look at the ring and realized she had seen it before. It was the 24k white gold diamond engagement ring she had picked out for her brother a few weeks ago. She was so excited when he told her he was going to propose to his girlfriend.

"I bet you're wondering how I have the same ring Cecil bought for Brandy," Tiffany hinted, noticing the confused look on Trinity's face. Trinity nodded. "Well, he actually has no intentions on proposing right now. I told him to tell you that because I knew you would pick out a ring you'd want." Trinity kissed Tiffany on the lips.

"You know me so well. We're getting married!" she yelled out happily and started jumping up and down some more. Trinity kissed Tiffany again and hugged her tightly. She was more than ready to spend the rest of her life with the woman she loved.

Lovers and Friends

It was late Saturday night, and Taj was lying down watching *Martin* when her cell phone startled her, blaring a loud notification. It was close to midnight, so she wondered who it was. Taj grabbed for her device slowly.

"Aw shit!" she yelled and jumped out of her bed like an Olympic sprinter. She was so excited because it was her crush, Roxi. Taj moved so quickly that she damn near tripped over her Nike slides. The message was vague but enough to make her heart race.

"Calm down, Taj," she coaxed herself out loud. She was way too excited, but if this was a booty call, she felt more than obliged to help Roxi out. She definitely didn't mind because she had been waiting a long time for this day to come.

Taj met Roxi through her cousin, Becca. The first time she laid eyes on Roxi, Taj was in awe. Roxi was so exotic looking. She was plainly dressed but seemed to have this glow about her, and her mocha skin was flawless. She had big brown eyes and full, pouty lips. Her hair was braided like Janet Jackson's was in the movie *Poetic Justice*, and she was twirling one of the braids with her finger while she talked. Taj had a thing for dark-skinned women, and Roxi was short too; that was another plus. Taj was 5'11", so a lot of women she hung around were shorter than she was. Even though she and Roxi clicked right away, Roxi had put Taj in the friend zone.

"Is it because I look like Ice Cube when he was on the heavier side?" Taj had asked jokingly. She did favor Ice Cube, but she had a more muscular physique and was a few shades lighter. Her emerald-colored eyes grew tight when she smiled.

"Are you kidding? That would be my number one reason for dating you," Roxi had replied, laughing. "Seriously though, I want to focus on school, and dating would be a complete distraction."

That was eight months ago. Now she was hitting Taj up in the middle of the night. Maybe Roxi wanted to finally move her out of the friend zone. Wait—Taj stopped herself. She was putting too much thought into a vague text message. She could have asked Roxi why she wanted her over, but Taj didn't want to sour the mood, if there was one.

She walked into her bathroom to wash her face and brush her teeth. She definitely didn't want to go over to Roxi's place with tart breath. Taj was kind of nervous, and that wasn't like her. She ran a comb through her hair and put it in a ponytail. She grabbed her backpack and took one more look in the mirror before she ran out the door and hopped in her car. Trey Songz' song, "Slow Motion," was playing on the radio. The lyrics were relatable because Taj was anticipating taking Roxi out of her clothes.

"Damn. I need to get my mind off sex," Taj mumbled once she made it to Roxi's. She couldn't seem to get out of the car; she was just sitting there looking crazy at one o'clock in the morning. Her hands felt so clammy.

"Alright, Taj. Pull yourself together," she coached herself. Taj took a deep breath and got out of her car. She took another deep breath before she rang the doorbell. When Roxi opened the door, Taj felt a tinge of disappointment. She thought Roxi would open the door wearing some boy shorts or lingerie, but Roxi was wearing a bonnet and one of those big night gowns like Taj's grandmother used to wear. Damn...so it wasn't a booty call.

"Hey, Mellow Yellow," Roxi sang, kissing Taj on the cheek. Taj wanted to let out a sigh. That was absolutely a friend-zone kiss. "I was having trouble sleeping, so I figured you wouldn't mind coming over and keeping me company. Exams kicked my ass this week. Do you want something to drink?"

Taj felt so freaking stupid. She should have known Roxi didn't have anything sexual in mind. Aside from their first time meeting, Roxi had never even flirted with Taj.

"Uh, a bottle of water, if you have some," Taj managed.

"Yeah, I do. You can sit down on the couch. I'm watching *Baby Boy*. I'll be right back," Roxi replied.

Roxi went into the kitchen and Taj slumped down on the couch. Of course, the movie was on the scene when Jody and Yvette were having sex...timing was not on Taj's side tonight. She didn't want to watch anyone get it in when she couldn't, even if they were only fictional characters. *Fuck!* She wanted to leave while Roxi was in the kitchen, but she wasn't that type of person. Roxi needed comforting from a friend, so Taj would give it to her.

"Taj?" Roxi had said her name so quietly Taj could barely hear her.

"Yeah," she answered with her eyes still glued to the TV.

"Look at me," Roxi instructed.

"Huh?" Taj asked, still frustrated and only half listening. She looked up and her mouth dropped open.

Roxi was standing in the doorway without the bonnet or the night gown. Instead, her hair was pulled up into a tight bun and she was wearing a red lace bra with matching lace panties. Roxi's skin was glowing like it had been when they first met. Taj was completely speechless.

"So, you're just going to sit there quietly?" Roxi teased with a whisper.

"Uh..." Taj was still at a loss for words.

"That's fine, love. We don't have to talk." Roxi walked over to the couch and sat sideways on Taj's lap. Taj snapped out of the daze she was in and planted a kiss on Roxi's lips. Roxi took it a step further, sliding her tongue inside Taj's mouth and kissing her passionately.

Taj scooped Roxi up and carried her into her bedroom.

"Are you sure you're ready for this?" she whispered, laying Roxi down gently on the bed.

Roxi didn't speak. She simply nodded and started the seduction of removing her lingerie. Taj was very nervous, but she kept her cool. It was finally about to happen, so she had to make sure she gave Roxi her all. She helped Roxi finish removing her lingerie and admired her naked body. It was perfect. Her mocha breasts were big and perky, and her nipples looked like they yearned to be sucked on. Even though Taj was anxious to get to Roxi's sweet spot, she knew it was necessary to start off with some foreplay. She started massaging Roxi's feet and then moved to her legs.

"That feels wonderful, but can we get to the good part?" Roxi interrupted with an enticing voice.

Taj didn't respond verbally. She just parted Roxi's legs and slowly rubbed her tongue up and down against Roxi's clit.

"*Yes!* I've been wanting this for too long!" Roxi said in a raspy voice. Her moaning and groaning turned Taj on even more. She started sucking on Roxi's clit while she slid her thumb inside Roxi. Roxi gyrated and moaned with pleasure as Taj moved her thumb in and out. Roxi tasted even better than Taj had imagined.

"Di-ddd you bring your strap?" Roxi managed to stutter between moans.

Taj nodded and gave Roxi's clit a sumptuous kiss before she got up. She was glad she had decided to grab it. Taj reached into her backpack and pulled out her brand new seven-inch dong. She was glad she had never used it before; Roxi was special to her. She knew this night wasn't only about sex.

"How do you want it, baby?" Taj whispered seductively after she fastened the harness.

Roxi smiled provocatively, spread her legs wide and pulled on her nipples. "I want you on top of me," she demanded.

Taj did as she was instructed, and Roxi moaned while she inserted the shaft. Once Taj was inside her, Roxi wrapped her legs around Taj, and Taj started stroking her slowly.

"Give me all you got. You don't have to be gentle. I like it rough," Roxi directed in a sensual voice.

Taj loved that Roxi was a talker. She hated when women didn't let it be known exactly what they wanted. Taj was usually good at recognizing body language, but she still wanted to know if what she was doing was pleasing to her partner. She did as she was told and sped up her strokes. She put Roxi's leg on her shoulder and went deeper into her love box.

"*Yes!* That's it! Keep fucking me like that!" Roxi screamed.

Her demands turned Taj on even more. She went as deep as she could, gripping the back of Roxi's legs.

Roxi dug her nails deep into Taj's back. She had a sex high and didn't want to come down. Taj was fucking her like this was a one-time thing. She didn't know it, but Roxi had called her over for more than a booty call. She was ready for a relationship with Taj. She just wanted Taj to fuck her brains out first before she let her know. Roxi had been interested in Taj for as long as Taj had been interested in her, but she didn't want to get into a new relationship while she was still sour about the last one.

"Ooh! Okay...okay! I can't take it anymore!" Roxi exclaimed with her legs still wrapped tightly around Taj's back.

"So, you want me to stop?" Taj whispered in her ear.

"No! Not yet...but slow down a little bit," Roxi let out barely above a whisper.

Taj decided to let Roxi take charge. Roxi kissed her tenderly on the lips and grabbed her waist to roll her onto her back. Now Roxi was on top. Roxi placed each of her hands on Taj's shoulders and started grinding on the shaft.

"Yes!" Roxi exclaimed, throwing her head back. Taj looked up at her. Roxi was biting her bottom lip. She rode the shaft for several minutes before peering into Taj's eyes longingly. Taj held her gaze. Both of them had the same thought—they should have done this sooner.

DESIRE

Brown Skin

Desire was lying in bed watching her girlfriend get undressed. They had been dating for almost three years, but the way Desire watched her, you'd think it was the first time she'd seen her naked.

Before Bailey came into her life, Desire felt as if she had a hole in her heart. Her soul was vacant, and she couldn't figure out a way to fill the void. She kept meeting women she was physically attracted to, but mentally, they weren't on her level. Because of that, Desire was never able to really connect with anyone enough to fall in love. She started to feel like she might be blindly sabotaging her relationships since they fizzled before they even started. What was it? Maybe love wasn't hers to enjoy.

Once Desire met Bailey, though, everything changed. The energy they shared was powerful right from the beginning. After six months of getting to know each other, their hugs turned into kisses and their friendship turned into a relationship. The transition from friendship to relationship happened so smoothly, they both thought it was too good to be true. The emptiness Desire thought had consumed her soul was now filled.

Bailey was a beautiful woman, but she didn't see her beauty in the way Desire saw it. Bailey was insecure about her smile and often talked about getting the gap closed between her two front teeth. Desire, however, absolutely loved her gap and always focused on Bailey's lips when she talked. The gap gave Bailey a distinct uniqueness that added to her beauty. Bailey thought of herself as average, but to Desire, she was so much more. She possessed more than outer beauty. She was beautiful on the inside as well. Bailey was a ray of sunshine and was passionate about life and those she loved. Desire was lucky to have her. She called her *ma belle âme,* which is French for "my beautiful soul."

"Hurry up, baby! I'm hungry," Desire commanded with a smirk.

Bailey strutted to the edge of the bed and slid one of her bra straps down seductively. She was a petite woman with breasts so large people would often ask her if she had implants, but they were natural.

"Oh, yeah? Well, I have something you can eat." Bailey smiled and showed her cute gap as she slowly unhooked her black satin bra and stepped out of her panties. She tossed them both on the floor and tauntingly did a three-sixty so Desire could continue to admire her. Desire's smile widened. She had her own personal model, and she loved it. Bailey had a fan for life when it came to Desire, even if she didn't realize it. She could really gaze at Bailey all day.

"My favorite meal." She got up from the bed, placed her hands around Bailey's slim waist and picked her up. Bailey wrapped her long legs around her. Desire could feel the warmth from her pussy, even though she was fully dressed. She didn't need to take off her own clothes because she planned on doing all the pleasing tonight. She laid Bailey on the bed gently and they kissed while Desire caressed her body. Bailey's skin was so soft Desire had to kiss every inch of her body each time they made love. Bailey certainly didn't mind being covered with her kisses. Desire always started from the base of her neck and worked her way down. Once she got to her juicy center, she inhaled deeply. The aroma of Bailey's pussy was tantalizing. Desire licked her lips with delight before French kissing Bailey's pussy. Bailey, in turn, placed her hands on top of Desire's head and pressed her face deeper into her pussy. Desire loved when she did that; it drove her wild. Her heart pounded rapidly in her chest. She stuck her tongue in as deep as it would go, and Bailey squeezed Desire's head tightly with her legs.

"Oooh! Yes, zaddy! Fuck me!" Bailey shouted and squeezed her head again.

Desire slowly slid two fingers inside of Bailey and moved them around while she gently sucked on her clit. Bailey squeezed her head once more. She was trying so hard not to scream, but Desire could tell that she really wanted to.

She pulled her fingers out and then stuck her tongue inside and started swirling it around.

"Oh, baby! That feels so good." Bailey moaned loudly as she came in Desire's mouth. Desire wasn't finished, though. Bailey's moans gave her motivation to make her come again, even harder, so she continued swirling her tongue around until Bailey couldn't take any more. "Ooh! Baby! I can't take it!" she cried out.

Desire took her tongue out but slid her fingers back inside. Bailey's creamy juices oozed out onto her fingers. She was coming again. "Do you want me to stop?" she asked in a low whisper but sped up her pace instead of slowing down.

"No, no, don't stop!" Bailey yelled, grabbing a fistful of Desire's hair.

"Ooh, okay! That's what I like to hear! You're so fucking wet, baby. I need to taste you again." Desire pulled her fingers out of Bailey's pussy and drove her tongue back inside of Bailey. More come seeped from between Bailey's legs. Desire tried to lap up all the juices like a thirsty dog. She lifted Bailey's ass so she would be able to slide her tongue from Bailey's clit to her chocolate starfish. Desire teased it with her finger before sticking her tongue inside of it. Bailey tried to reach for Desire's hair again but ended up gripping the sheets instead. Desire continued to tongue-fuck Bailey until her face was saturated in Bailey's juices.

BECCA

Teen Spirit

Have you ever wanted to give in completely to satisfaction, but you knew once you relaxed, the orgasm that followed might be too overwhelming for you to handle? That was Becca's current dilemma. The pleasure was overwhelming. She was straddling cloud nine and didn't want Lexi to know she had her completely sprung—the type of sprung that would make her call off of work so she could get in another "quickie." She would miss out on making money to get her sexual desires fulfilled. It was hard for Becca to act nonchalant about the way she was feeling because, with each tongue stroke, her body shook uncontrollably. She bit down hard on her bottom lip to hold back the scream that almost escaped. She had to tighten her legs around Lexi's head in order to keep her composure.

Lexi could tell that Becca was holding back, and she was determined to get her to let loose. She slid her fingers inside Becca's already soaking wet pussy, moving them in and out swiftly while sucking on her clit. Lexi glanced up at Becca and saw that she had her eyes closed and her lips slightly parted. She sucked Becca's clit and then slid her tongue inside of her. Becca's body trembled as her juices oozed into Lexi's mouth. Even while swallowing every drop, Lexi continued to tongue-fuck Becca vigorously.

"Ah!" she moaned loudly. "Fuck, yeah! This feels so fucking good!" Becca screamed while gripping a fistful of Lexi's hair. She could no longer remain silent. Her body shook some more and she yelled out again. Lexi loved that she was finally being vocal. She sucked on Becca's clit a little bit harder, and Becca tightened her grip on her hair. She was having an out-of-body experience, and she didn't want it to end.

"Where the hell have you been hiding?!" Becca yelled out while panting.

Lexi laughed quietly but didn't say anything. She just continued to stroke her hungrily. She planned on eating Becca's pussy until she couldn't take it anymore.

Creep

Nola couldn't stop staring at her houseguest. She had never been attracted to a woman before, but there was something about Rae that had her slightly intrigued. Maybe it was her dreads. They fit her slender face perfectly. They were in the beginning stages, but Rae wore them well. Or maybe it was how she dressed: GQ mixed with a little hood. No, it was her accent. Rae had a slightly raspy voice with a Creole drawl. Nola could listen to her talk all day. She really wanted to get to know Rae on an intimate level, but she wasn't going to let her know that. Nola couldn't let her know because she had a boyfriend—a fiancé to be exact. Lately, things hadn't been going well between them, but that wasn't a good reason for Nola to be lusting over a woman. Was she lusting? She wasn't sure exactly what to call her infatuation, but she had been feeling this way for a few weeks now. The longer Nola went without having sex, the more she fantasized about having sex with Rae. Well, truth be told, she had also been fantasizing about Rae while she was having sex with her man. Nola got goosebumps every time she and Rae were in the same room together. The way Rae looked at her set her soul on fire. Nola wanted her badly.

Rae had met Nola through her cousin, Asia, and when she needed to get away from her previous living situation, Nola told Rae she could stay with her and her fiancé until she was able to get on her feet again. Rae had known Nola for about six months and had been living with her and her fiancé for about three months. Nola had a nurturing demeanor about her. She was the type of person who would help someone out and wouldn't expect to receive anything in return. Rae liked Nola right off the bat. She could tell Nola was interested because she caught Nola checking her out a few times. She was still trying to debate whether she wanted to make a move or not. Nola was ten years older than Rae, but Rae didn't care about Nola's age. She also didn't care about her being engaged because things weren't popping in their bedroom like they should have been. The entire time she had lived with the couple, she had only heard them having sex once. The moans Nola made were so mediocre that it was clear she was faking. Nola had revealed to Rae that she no longer found her fiancé, Sean, attractive; they were basically holding on by a thread. He had become too comfortable in their relationship and was not the romantic man he used to be. As soon as he got off of work, he would come home, eat and then tune in to the TV for the remainder of the night.

Rae listened to Nola vent about Sean, but she never

offered any advice because she had none to give. She wanted to fuck Nola, so why pretend to have compassion for her relationship woes? She wasn't going to make any advances, but if Nola ever decided to cross the line, Rae would be ready. Rae's body language showed that she was interested, but she never expressed it verbally; she was kind of skeptical when it came to Nola. Nola had never been with a woman before, so Rae knew if she fucked her, she would probably end up with a pillow princess. Or she would have to teach Nola how to eat pussy, and she didn't feel like doing that.

Nola looked over at her fiancé, Sean, who was snoring so loudly he woke her up. She groaned and nudged him to get him to roll over and shut up. He grunted and turned onto his side.

"Finally," Nola mumbled, rolling her eyes. Sean had always snored, but lately, every little thing he did annoyed her. She was so tired of him. She picked up her cell phone to look at the time. It was two-thirty. She had only drifted off to sleep an hour ago. She groaned and put the phone back down. This was her life, and she wasn't happy. What would make her happy?

Since Sean was no longer satisfying her, she would do it herself. Nola pulled her panties off and started caressing her pussy. She parted her legs and then slid two fingers inside of her aching pussy. After a few angry strokes, she realized she didn't want to please herself. She looked back over at Sean and groaned again. She wasn't about to wake him up, knowing full well he wasn't going to get the job done. He had become such a selfish lover.

She wondered if their houseguest was awake. She laid there for several minutes longer until her curiosity got the best of her. Maybe it was time for her to make a daring move. She eased out of bed and crept towards the bedroom door. She looked back at Sean one last time before turning the knob. Her heart was beating fast as she eased down the staircase.

Rae was sitting on the couch watching TV. She didn't see Nola until she stepped out of the shadows. Rae's mouth dropped open. Nola was standing in front of her in a t-shirt, without any panties on. Her shaved pussy looked delectable. "Can you fuck me please?" Nola pleaded, even though it was more of a demand.

"Hell yeah! Come here, girl!" Rae exclaimed.

Nola strolled over to the couch. Nola's body language read confidence, but her mind was beyond on edge. Not only was this her first time having sex with a woman, she had a man sleeping upstairs. She felt bad, but not bad enough to walk away from Rae.

"I've been wanting to give you some dick so bad. Is that what you want, ma? You want me to fuck you like you need to be fucked?" Rae wasn't looking in Nola's eyes when she asked the questions. She wasn't talking to Nola at all. She was talking to Nola's pussy. It was shaved bare, and her clit was pierced. Rae didn't have to imagine what Nola's pussy looked like anymore. She knew she needed to taste Nola before she strapped up. She grabbed Nola by the waist and pulled her close. "I want you to stand up and spread your legs open wide for me."

Nola spread her legs and Rae got down on her knees directly in front of Nola's pussy. She slid her middle finger inside Nola and slowly started rubbing her tongue up and down Nola's clit. Nola put her hands on Rae's shoulders and threw her head back. Rae's tongue felt so good she wanted to scream. Rae continued until her face was soaking wet with Nola's juices. She got up off of her knees and wiped her mouth. "Lay down on the couch; I'm about to get my strap. Well, I should say *your* strap. I bought a new one just for you. The sexual tension between us has been building, so I knew you would eventually give me some pussy." She giggled in Nola's ear.

Nola shuddered and lay on the couch and waited for Rae to put the strap on. Rae climbed on top of Nola and slowly eased her way inside of Nola's pussy. Nola tightened her muscles and froze up.

"Relax. I'm going to be gentle...this time," Rae told her reassuringly.

Nola relaxed her body and wrapped her legs around Rae's back. Rae gripped Nola's thighs, stroking her slowly. Nola moaned quietly. She never would have guessed that a fake dick could feel so good. Her whole body seemed to vibrate.

Rae started kissing Nola's neck and titties. She wished they could have had sex in Nola's king-sized bed. The couch was comfortable, but she needed more space. "I want you to get up and stand against the wall. I'm going to pick you up."

Nola raised an eyebrow and frowned skeptically. "You're a little small. You sure you can lift me up?"

"Hell yeah. Don't let my petite size fool you," Rae replied, laughing. "I'm cock strong."

Nola did as she was instructed. Rae sized Nola up as she stood in front of her. Rae smirked and squatted so she could slide the dong inside of her.

"Wrap your legs around my back," she directed. As soon as Nola wrapped her legs around Rae's back, Rae gripped Nola's thighs and moved back away from the wall. She bounced Nola up and down. Nola dug her long nails into Rae's shoulders. She forgot they weren't alone and let her moans get louder. Rae laid her down on the carpet and continued to stroke her. She placed a hand over Nola's mouth and stroked a little faster until they both came. Rae got off of Nola and lay on the floor. Nola wanted more. She climbed on top of Rae and started riding the dong. Nola leaned forward and gripped the carpet.

"Fuck! We're definitely doing this again!" Nola bounced up and down vigorously until she came. She gave Rae a peck on the lips and slid off of her.

Without any final words, she ascended the stairs and crept back into her bedroom. Sean was still knocked out and snoring. She was tempted to go back downstairs to Rae again but decided against it. Nola went into her bathroom and started the shower. While washing her body, she thought about how good Rae had fucked her. She was going to fuck Rae again as soon as Sean left for work.

MICAH

Vapors

Micah felt like she was the only stud in the call center, the way all the women came on to her. Maybe it was because she was tall, chocolate and muscular. Her eyes were as dark as coal. You would get lost gazing into them. Micah kept her jet black hair cut low and had waves deeper than the ocean. She had only been working at the call center for three months, yet she had received an array of gifts and unexpected surprises. At first it was flattering, but now it was starting to feel like sexual harassment. At least three days a week, Micah would get off work and find a note on her windshield. Yesterday, someone went as far as leaving a pair of panties in her desk drawer with a note that read, *"I'd really love if you'd take these off for me next time. Xoxo."* Whoever the pantyless woman was, she didn't sign her name. All Micah knew from looking at the panties was that the woman who left them was probably slim. She had nothing against slender women, but they weren't really her cup of tea. She only dated women with lots of curves and love handles. Micah's ex-girlfriend, Shante, was five-eleven and two hundred pounds of gorgeousness. That relationship had lasted for three years.

Everything had been going fine until Micah told Shante she wanted to move. Micah didn't want to grow old in their small hometown, but Shante had wanted to stay put. Micah had suggested they try to commit to a long-distance relationship, but Shante was as stubborn as a mule. There was no such thing as a compromise with her. She told Micah if she moved, they were breaking up. Micah loved Shante and had made sacrifices for their relationship in the past, but she wasn't about to sacrifice her happiness. She knew she would end up resenting Shante if she stayed, so they broke up and Micah moved away.

The first month they were apart, Micah thought she was going to lose her mind. She felt as if she had given up her whole world. She missed Shante badly, but their chapter was over, according to Shante. Micah needed to move on. She didn't want to jump into a new relationship, but she did crave some female company, even if it was only to cuddle. Micah had gotten used to sleeping next to a woman every night and then, wham! Single life. The problem she was having now was that none of the women who came on to her really wanted to get to know her. They just wanted to fuck. The panties in Micah's desk proved just how bold their efforts were. Now, don't get it twisted; Micah loved sex. She just wasn't into random hookups anymore. She had been a little wild before she met Shante. Once Shante came along, she realized that a meaningful relationship was a good thing, and because of that and many other things, Shante would always have a piece of Micah's heart. Reminiscing about her made Micah feel some type of way. Maybe a random hookup would make her feel a little better. Nah, she knew it wouldn't. Micah kind of wanted to move back to her hometown and try to get back with Shante, but then she would still be only partially happy. She decided to call and see if Shante was willing to fly in for a visit. Micah would pay for her flight without hesitation.

"Hey, Shante. I was worried you wouldn't answer. How are you doing?"

Shante sighed loudly before replying, "I thought about letting it ring, but then I decided to go ahead and answer. I'm okay...considering my girlfriend left me." Even though Shante answered the phone on the first ring, she was not going to give Micah any slack.

"Shante, that's not fair. Why would you make me feel guilty for leaving, when I didn't want to leave without you?"

There was silence on the line. Shante was still mad at Micah, but she also missed her. She wanted Micah to feel guilty, even though she knew she shouldn't have been pressed. Micah had told her she wanted a change in scenery long before she moved away by herself. Shante was also sad that she and Micah didn't fight hard enough for their relationship. Micah really tried to make it work, but Shante was so headstrong she let Micah slip away. Even now that she had Micah on the phone, she was too proud to tell

Micah how she really felt. The day Micah left and many days after, Shante cried herself to sleep. She wanted to be with Micah but was scared of such a drastic change. What if she had moved too, only to break up later?

"Well, you shouldn't have left me. What do you want?"

"I want you to come visit me for the weekend," Micah replied. "You never know; you might like it here and decide to move."

"Nah, I'm good."

Micah's heart sank, but she was determined to win Shante back. Even though Shante was being an abrupt asshole, Micah could tell that she missed her, too. "I'm going to text you my address. If you change your mind, I'm off every weekend."

"Bye, Micah."

"Damn. Well, I tried."

Shante didn't have any final words. She just ended the call. Micah sat and stared at the wall. That's not how she expected the phone call to go. She knew Shante wasn't going to give in easily, but she didn't think their conversation would be so short. Micah wanted Shante to understand where she was coming from, but she hadn't thought about how Shante felt. Maybe they would reunite one day. Micah could only hope.

A year had passed since the breakup. Micah and Shante

talked on the phone often, but Shante still hadn't come to visit. Micah liked that they were communicating, but she was crushed when Shante told her she was dating and would likely never come visit. Micah had known Shante would start dating eventually, but she didn't want to know about it. Shante reminded Micah that, as friends, they should be willing to talk about any and everything, just like they did when they were together. There was a big difference between then and now for Micah, though.

Once, Shante had asked Micah if she ever wanted to have a threesome, and Micah told her no without hesitation. She wasn't looking for anything extra, and she wasn't trying to share. Now that she was single, she had the opportunity to sleep with whomever she wanted. She had come really close to sleeping with one of the coworkers she had been chopping it up with, but when it came time, she chickened out. After making love to Shante for so long, Micah couldn't picture herself with another woman. Shante, on the other hand, was letting some random stud eat her pussy from the back. She hadn't told Micah that she had slept with anyone, but her demeanor was different whenever she and Micah facetimed. Micah wanted to ask Shante but didn't really want to know the answer.

But now Micah was at home on a Friday night, letting the TV watch her. She was supposed to be hanging out with a few of her friends but didn't feel like being social. She had told herself she was going to make it a movie night, but she was too busy looking at old videos and pictures of her and

Shante. She was halfway through the second photo album when there was a knock at the door.

"Ugh! Leave me alone. I don't feel like being bothered tonight." Micah huffed, trudging to the door. She knew it was her friends coming to drag her out with them. Micah took a look through the peephole, but whoever it was decided to block the hole with their finger. She chuckled to herself. Her goofy friends were here to cheer her up. She opened the door and her jaw dropped.

"Are you going to let me in or are you going to stand there gaping at me?" Shante asked with a smirk. Micah was still speechless. This couldn't be real; she had to be dreaming. Chills ran through her body. It had been a whole year since she'd laid eyes on Shante, not counting their FaceTime calls. "I was in the neighborhood and decided to pop up on yo' ass. Did I catch you at a bad time?"

Micah knew damn well Shante wasn't just in the neighborhood. She had caught a flight with one purpose, and that was to see Micah.

She was wearing her *"Girl, you got this"* sexy cropped sweater—the one she had bought from an online store called Pretty Little Thing. Shante figured Micah would be at home, even though when they spoke earlier in the day, Micah had told her she was going out with friends. Shante could tell by Micah's tone that she wasn't going anywhere. Shante was glad she had been right. Otherwise, she would have had to call Micah and ruin the surprise.

"Of course, not! I'm just shocked to see you here!" Micah

exclaimed. She grabbed Shante and kissed her passionately. To Micah, it seemed like they hadn't locked lips in ages. Shante's lips were still so soft and luscious. She wrapped her arms around Shante and held onto her tightly. After a few minutes of embracing, she let go. "Let me take your bag. Come on in."

Shante was trying hard to mask her excitement. She was playing cool, even though she wanted to jump into Micah's arms the moment she opened the door. Truth is, she'd tried dating other women after they split, but she hadn't met anyone that stimulated her mind the way Micah did. On top of that, Micah was the first woman and the only woman to pick her up. She always lifted Shante off the ground like she was a mere hundred pounds. She quivered just thinking about it.

Micah noticed the quiver but didn't mention it. "Take a seat on the couch. You want something to drink? You're still so beautiful, by the way."

Shante blushed. "No, thank you. I'm not thirsty. You look good, too."

"I can't believe you came. What about your lil' boo thang?" Micah asked in a mocking tone.

"You know it's hard for me to do vulnerability, but I've been missing you since the day you left. I didn't want to tell you because I felt that would be the weak thing to do. I wanted you to continue to beg me to come, and that was stupid and selfish. I can admit when I've been foolish. I tried to get over you by dating other women, but they couldn't keep me interested. There are a lot of lames out there. I've been stupid and stubborn for entirely too long. I want you back, Micah, if you'll still have me."

"It's about damn time," Micah replied, laughing. "Of course, I will still have you. I've been waiting for you to tell me that."

Shante stood up and pulled her crop top off. She was wearing a mesh bra underneath and her nipples were pushing through the fabric. Micah licked her lips. She was ready to kiss, lick and suck on the luscious mounds. If she had a dick, it would have been rock hard. She shifted to the edge of the couch and pulled Shante to her. She unbuttoned Shante's pants and rolled them down slowly. Once Micah got them off, she rubbed the outside of Shante's panties. Her large clit looked like it wanted to bust through them. Micah threw her head back and howled like a wolf. She felt like a beast was trapped inside of her, the way her heart was pounding.

Shante grabbed Micah's hair with both hands and massaged her scalp. She was surprised Micah had decided to grow it out. She bit her bottom lip. Micah was teasing her, so Shante decided she should do some teasing as well. Micah got tired of the teasing game quickly and ripped Shante's panties off to thrust her tongue deep inside Shante's pussy.

"Ooh, baby! Yes, I need you to eat this muthafucking pussy!" Shante moaned, throwing her head back. Her legs felt weak and she knew she would have buckled if Micah hadn't been holding her up.

Shante tasted so good that Micah's pussy was pulsating.

She wanted to get Shante to the bedroom so she could tongue-fuck her on the bed instead of the couch. Micah ran her tongue across Shante's clit before she stood up.

"Come on, baby. I'm about to fuck you so good you won't be able to do anything afterwards."

"Ooh, yes, daddy! I need that kind of fucking in my life," Shante purred as she followed Micah to the bedroom. Once they made it through the door, Micah unhooked Shante's bra and tossed it to the floor. She squeezed Shante's breasts and then pulled at her nipples. Shante shuddered.

"Lay down on the bed. I'm about to strap up," Micah directed, slapping Shante hard on the ass. Shante loved when Micah was rough with her. She lay down on the bed and watched Micah pull her bag of dicks out the closet. Micah had dicks of different sizes because she wanted Shante to feel something different each time she fucked her. She pulled out her harness and her eight-inch dong. She was about to give Shante's fat pussy the business! Shante was propped up on her elbows watching her tall and stocky love with intensity and anticipation.

Damn, she's so fine, Shante thought. Her pussy was tingling just watching Micah.

"I was going to get on top, but I want you to ride me," Micah told Shante after she finished putting on her harness.

"Whatever you want me to do, baby. Lie down," Shante whispered while repositioning herself. Micah lay down so Shante could climb on top of her. Shante rubbed the tip of the dong across her already wet clit. That really turned

Micah on, even though she couldn't feel it. Shante slowly eased down on top of the dong and bounced up and down.

"Ooh, yes! Yes, baby! You betta ride this motherfucker! Damn, I missed your fat-ass pussy!" Micah was moaning and yelling so loud her neighbors could probably hear her through the walls. She didn't care, though.

"This pussy missed you too, baby!"

"I don't want to be without you!" Micah cried out. She had never felt so emotional during sex. Absence really does make the heart grow fonder. She grabbed Shante's waist and stood up. She kept the dong inside Shante as she laid her down on the bed, spreading Shante's legs wide while she stroked her. Shante dug her nails into Micah's arms and moaned louder with each stroke. Neither of them wanted their lovemaking to end. They fucked until they could barely breathe.

"Damn, baby, that was so good," Shante said, panting.

Micah nodded and clapped. She couldn't have agreed more. That was the best sex they had ever had. More importantly, she had gotten her heart back. She kissed Shante on the forehead and they drifted off to sleep.

RAYNE

Harem

It had been a drawn-out, tiring day for Rayne, so she was more than anxious to get home and take a long, hot shower. She was exhausted, to say the least, and glad it was Friday because she didn't work the weekend. She was starving and wanted to grab something to eat, but she knew there would be a plate in the oven waiting for her when she got home, so Rayne decided to ignore the rumbling in her stomach. That home-cooked meal would be much better than grabbing fast food anyway. For the past three years, she had worked so many hours every week that she never had to cook or clean. That was one of the many perks of being in a happy relationship. Rayne was spoiled, but she made sure she did some spoiling as well.

When she walked into their home, it was pitch black inside. Rayne flipped the light switch and walked into the empty kitchen. She opened the oven and, as predicted, there was her food. She pulled the plate from the oven and pulled back the foil. It was her favorite meal: lasagna, green beans and garlic bread. It was still warm.

"Ooh, this is going to be so good," she said. Right as Rayne was about to grab a fork, she heard loud moans coming from the bedroom. She raised an eyebrow and put her plate down, no longer interested in eating. Rayne crept down the hallway towards the bedroom and opened the door. She stood in the doorway and didn't say a word. She only watched.

Simone's eyes were closed, and her hands cuffed her breasts as she rode Gia's face slowly. Gia was gripping the back of Simone's thigh with one hand and fingering herself with the other. Gia was a good multitasker. Rayne watched the scene, excited. Simone opened her eyes briefly and saw Rayne standing in the doorway. "Come join us, baby," she breathed, extending her arms.

Rayne smiled. "I barely made it through the door, and I haven't taken a shower yet."

Simone stopped riding Gia's face and slid off the bed. Gia followed, and they stepped over to Rayne so they could undress her. Rayne didn't resist; she let them have their way with her.

Rayne had been in a relationship with Gia for a year before they met Simone. They had discussed being a poly couple prior to meeting her. It was Gia's idea, and Rayne was open to it. They agreed that Gia, the bolder of the two, should be the one to find their additional girlfriend. By chance, Gia met Simone through a mutual friend. Gia and

Rayne got to know her as a friend, and later, once Simone was comfortable around them, they asked her how she felt about being in a relationship with them. She was open to it and was a perfect fit.

Poly relationships weren't for everyone, but for the last two years, it had been everything for them. A relationship that some might see as weird or freaky was very normal for the three of them. It was deeper than just having a threesome; it was about having a real connection. Intimacy wasn't the most important aspect of their relationship—communication was. Since they made sure they communicated all of their issues and concerns, there wasn't any jealousy or animosity among the women.

Once Rayne was completely undressed, they brought her to the king-sized bed. Rayne sat on the edge and grabbed Gia's hand and kissed it, repeating the action for Simone. She couldn't help but look at her partners and smile. She was lucky to share her physical and mental space with these two beautiful souls. Rayne kissed Simone's full lips and then kissed Gia's.

"Lie back, baby," Simone directed, pushing Rayne backward playfully. Rayne did what she was told, and Simone climbed on top of her. Her faux locs dangled in front of her face as she leaned forward until their breasts were touching. Rayne slipped her tongue into Simone's mouth, and while they were kissing, Gia slid behind Simone to plant kisses on her neck and shoulders. Simone sat up to grind her clit against Rayne's warm, wet pussy.

"Ahhh!" Rayne moaned and squeezed her thighs. Simone smiled seductively and continued to ride Rayne's clit vigorously. Gia climbed onto the bed, squatting over Rayne so Rayne could tongue-fuck her from behind. Rayne grabbed Gia's ass and brushed her tongue up against Gia's clit, hooking her thumb to slide it inside her pussy while massaging her asshole with her middle finger.

"Oh, fuck! Yes, baby!" Gia squealed with delight. Rayne bit Gia's ass playfully. Gia moaned and put her hands on Simone's shoulders; her legs were about to give out. Rayne saw Gia trembling and pulled Gia's pussy directly on top of her face. She gripped Gia's ass cheeks while continuing to devour her. Gia wanted to kiss and rub on Simone, but the way Rayne was twirling her tongue around inside Gia's pussy, she could barely move. *"Oh, yes!"* she yelled, releasing all her juices in Rayne's mouth. Gia's body quaked and she rolled off of Rayne's face to collapse next to her partners. Simone giggled and pinched Gia's thigh.

"I'm all tapped out, baby," Gia panted with her eyes closed. Simone laughed and kissed Rayne's stomach, still sitting on top of her. She slowly inched her way to the head of the bed so she could take her turn riding Rayne's face. Rayne was ready. She gripped the back of Simone's thighs as Simone gyrated on her tongue. Simone only lasted a few seconds before coming in Rayne's mouth. She slid off of Rayne and lay with half her body across Gia's. Rayne kissed them both on the lips, letting them taste their mixed juices.

Rayne got up and made her way to the kitchen. She was

parched and needed a Gatorade, not to mention the meal she had left. By the time she walked back to the bedroom, both her beauties were snuggled under the covers sound asleep. She climbed in bed with them, happy to end her work week.

TATI

Say Yes

Tati sat in her car outside her friend Sarah's house with her hands tightly clutching the steering wheel. She had been sitting there for ten minutes and wanted to get out, but she was too nervous. She looked down at her palms. They were sweating profusely, so she wiped them on her tights. She hadn't planned on sweating before she made it into the party, but her nerves were completely shot. Well, at least she had made sure she put on an outfit that showed off her curves to perfection. She glanced over at Sarah's house for the third time and still wasn't sure if she wanted to go inside. She had decided to ditch the date she was going to bring to the party. It had been too long since she last saw Nevaeh, and she wasn't going to be ignored tonight.

The last time they were together, the tension was so thick you couldn't cut it with a knife. They had been friends, then lovers, and now they were strangers. Tati's heart ached for the loss of their friendship. Nevaeh had said she would always be part of Tati's life, but things hadn't worked out that way. Tati looked at the house again and sighed. She would get out of the car eventually, but right now she just wanted to sit in her car and wallow. The radio was playing with the volume low, but when she heard Musiq Soulchild singing, Tati had to turn it up. "Half Crazy"…that song really depicted how she felt right then. Part of her wanted to cry. Why did things go south between them? She switched the radio off and took a deep breath. Tati couldn't talk to Nevaeh if she stayed in her car all night. It was now or never. She checked her appearance one last time and then got out of her car. It was a cool night, but Tati was still sweating as she walked to the door and tapped on it lightly.

"Who is it?" Tati recognized the voice immediately. It was Nevaeh. She was disguising her voice playfully, but Tati could tell it was her. She felt a knot of nervousness turning in her stomach.

"Uh. It's me, Tati."

"Who?" Nevaeh asked, laughing as she opened the door. The negative tension Tati had expected was surprisingly absent.

"Hey, where is everybody?" Tati asked. Her heart was racing, and she couldn't understand why Nevaeh still had that effect on her. She caught a whiff of Nevaeh's perfume and wanted to wrap her arms around Nevaeh's neck and kiss her.

"They're outside on the patio. I just came in to refill my drink," Nevaeh replied, raising the red Solo cup to her lips.

Why did she look sexy, even while she was drinking from a plastic cup? Damn. Tati really wanted to give her a big hug.

"I need to get in on that. It's trashcan punch?"

"Yup." Nevaeh took another sip. She was staring at Tati silently. Tati wanted to spark up a conversation with her then, but she decided to wait. She poured herself a cup of punch and took a sip. It was strong but so good. She planned on having more than one cup tonight.

Nevaeh headed outside, and Tati followed. Sarah and about six of their mutual friends were all sitting around smoking, laughing and drinking. Tati hugged everyone and took a seat on the porch swing. She joined the conversation, but mostly, she was trying not to stare at Nevaeh. She looked good enough to eat, and it wasn't only the alcohol that had Tati feeling warm.

"Earth to T!" Sarah hollered, clapping her hands. "Did you hear anything I said?"

"Huh?" Tati was jolted from her daydreams. She was deeper in thought than she had realized and hadn't even heard Sarah call her name.

"Girl, I'm so stoned right now. I was in my own world. What'd you say?" Tati asked, knowing full well that she wasn't close to being high yet.

"I said we should take it in the house and have you plug your phone into the TV. You know you're the honorary DJ!" They all laughed as they got up and headed inside. Tati connected her phone to Sarah's TV and turned her music on. She took another sip of her drink. Even though she was amongst friends and there wasn't any tension between Nevaeh and her tonight, Tati was still nervous. She finished her drink and refilled her cup. She took a seat on one of the recliners and bopped her head to the music. When Ty Dolla Sign's song, "Like I Do" came on, Tati got up and started dancing, trying not to watch Nevaeh, who was sitting on the couch with their friend, Ana.

Tati felt like Nevaeh was watching her, but she wasn't a hundred percent sure because she was trying hard not to make eye contact. For a moment, Tati thought Nevaeh and Ana might have been talking about her, but she wasn't sure. She turned her back to them and continued dancing.

"Why don't you give her a lap dance, T?" Ana asked, catching Tati off guard. She turned back around and smiled shyly.

"Huh?" Tati asked, as if she hadn't heard Ana's suggestion.

"Lap dance! Lap dance! Lap dance!" everyone in the room chanted in unison. Tati hadn't realized anyone else had been paying attention to the conversation until they chimed in. Nevaeh half smiled and repositioned herself on the couch but didn't say anything.

"Look at y'all being messy," Tati replied, laughing. As tempted as Tati was to succumb to the pressure of her peers, she took a moment to think about it. Being that close and personal was definitely something that Tati wanted, but fear of rejection kept her from doing any of it. Being rejected by Nevaeh wouldn't feel good at all, so she decided it was best to keep her distance. Besides, she knew that if she did take that leap into Nevaeh's personal space, she would want to take things further than a grind on her thighs. So instead, Tati chose a way out.

"I'm about to refill my cup and fix me a plate," she said, preparing her exit. "Anybody want something while I'm in the kitchen?"

"You can refill my cup if you want," Nevaeh said, holding up her cup. Tati felt a sudden rush of warmth flow through her as her eyes met Nevaeh's. She reached out to take the cup being offered.

"You got it. I'll be right back," she told her. In the kitchen, Tati took several deep breaths to sedate the butterflies she suddenly felt fluttering in her stomach. *Focus,* she told herself. *The last thing you want is to drop the drink and look crazy. Just relax,* she inwardly coached.

Back in the living room, Tati extended Navaeh's drink to her, trying hard not to react when their fingers brushed lightly. Tati smiled and went back into the kitchen. She fixed herself a plate of nachos and refilled her cup again, before sitting back down on the recliner. Before she knew it, Tati had emptied her cup again. She usually didn't drink this much, but tonight she needed to be as loose as possible. When Ana came and sat next to her, Tati wanted to have a conversation, but it was hard for her to focus. It felt like the whole room was vibrating. She was definitely drunk. Tati put her empty cup on the floor, took off her shoes and pulled her feet up under her body. She sat there for a while, barely noticing the scene around her. Sarah retired to her room, and their other friends slowly started leaving one by one. Soon, it was only Tati and Nevaeh left in the living room.

"Are you going home?" Nevaeh asked with her eyes barely open.

"I had too much to drink, so I'm going to lie here for a while."

"Yeah, me too." Nevaeh said, closing her eyes.

Tati drifted off, and when she woke up, it was five a.m. She looked over at Nevaeh, who was curled up in a ball, sound asleep. Tati thought about leaving, but she didn't want to go before having a real conversation with Nevaeh. Still tipsy, Tati thought a shower might help her wake up. She knew Sarah wouldn't mind.

Tati, sleepy and tipsy, had been in the shower for about twenty minutes. She was mumbling to herself, "I didn't think this through. I don't have any clothes to put on." She didn't want to bother Sarah, since it was still early. Since she was going to be there for a while, she decided to throw her clothes in the washer. She grabbed a large towel from the linen closet and had just started wrapping the towel around her body when she heard a light tap on the door.

"Tati?" It was Nevaeh whispering from the other side.

Tati's heart was racing. Instead of responding, she opened the door slowly. "Uh...yeah?" she asked nervously, the towel loosely covering her wet body.

"I wanted to check on you to make sure you're okay." Nevaeh sounded nervous as well.

"I'm good, but, uh..." Tati's voice trailed off and they stared at each other for a few seconds in silence.

"But what?" Nevaeh asked and slid her hands underneath the towel to cuff Tati's waist. She wasn't cold, but a chill ran through her as soon as Nevaeh's hands rested on her body. Tati shuddered and let the towel drop to the floor as she leaned in to kiss Nevaeh's neck. They had so much they needed to talk about, but Tati wasn't interested in discussing any of it at the moment. She rested her head against Nevaeh's chest and felt her heart racing. They stood there for several moments in silence wrapped up in each other's arms.

"I know you just got out the shower, but do you want to get back in?" Nevaeh whispered in her ear.

Instead of a verbal reply, Tati pulled Nevaeh's joggers down. Once Nevaeh was completely undressed, they climbed into the shower and turned the water back on. Nevaeh's back was to the shower, and Tati gazed up into her eyes, watching the beads of water trickle down Nevaeh's shoulders. She was so damn sexy.

"What are you thinking about?" Nevaeh asked, putting her hand under Tati's chin and tilting her head back.

Tati hesitated and then smiled. "I'm thinking about you, me...the old us. We used to have so much fun together, but things changed overnight. How could you go from sharing everything with me to completely ghosting me?" Tati bit her bottom lip and put her head down. "That really hurt. I'm still hurting behind our breakup."

Nevaeh gently tilted Tati's head back up and kissed her

gently on her lips. "Let me officially apologize for the pain I caused you. I never meant to hurt you. I was battling some personal demons, and instead of talking to the woman I loved, I pushed you away. I promise to never leave you out in the cold like that again. Can we start over?"

Tati smiled, "Yes. I'd love that." Nevaeh wrapped her hands around Tati's waist and kissed her again, this time more passionately. They completely disregarded the fact that they were in someone else's house. "Put your foot on the side of the tub," Nevaeh whispered in Tati's ear and then licked her earlobe.

Tati could barely keep her composure. She lifted her leg slowly to rest her foot on the side of the tub. Nevaeh slipped a single finger inside Tati, sliding in and out of her wetness. Tati's back arched at the sensation. "Ooh...yes..." she crooned. "I've missed you so much, baby."

Nevaeh briefly closed her eyes and bit her bottom lip. Tati rested her head on Nevaeh's breast and dug her nails deep into her back. Nevaeh grasped Tati's right thigh, continuing to pleasure her. "I love you so much," Tati confessed.

"I love you more," Nevaeh moaned, pulling her fingers from her lover and preparing to savor Tati's juices. Before Nevaeh could get her fingers to her mouth, Tati grabbed Nevaeh's hand and sucked the juices from her fingers. "That was supposed to be for me." Nevaeh smiled.

"I got more where that came from…" Tati teased.

The water was starting to get cold, but they didn't mind

one bit. Nevaeh cupped Tati's breasts and planted kisses on them. She looked into Tati's eyes and held her gaze for a few moments in silence. They would hold on to this moment forever.

SYDNEY

Drown in It

For the longest time, Tisha had made it abundantly clear that she wasn't looking for a relationship. At first, Syd was fine with only being friends, but the more time they spent together, the more she wanted to get to know Tisha on a more intimate level.

When Syd had first told Tisha how she felt, Tisha had rejected her, saying a sexual relationship would more than likely ruin their friendship. It had happened to Tisha before, and she didn't want to lose another friend over a failed sexual connection. Syd respected Tisha's wishes and fell back. Even though she wanted something to happen between them, she didn't want Tisha to feel uncomfortable around her. She knew having Tisha as a friend was more valuable than sex.

At least once a week, Tisha would come over to Syd's place, and they would watch movies on Netflix. Syd was searching for something for them to watch when Tisha rang her doorbell. She got up from the couch and rushed to open the door. Tisha had a big smile plastered on her face.

"Happy to see me, huh?"

"After the crap day I had, I am in dire need of a friend," Tisha replied, dramatically throwing her head back and placing the back of her hand on her forehead.

"Well, you came to the right place." Syd gave Tisha a warm hug and pulled her inside. "Pull off your shoes so we can sit down on the couch and you can tell me all about your day. So, what happened?"

"Nothing. I just felt like being extra," Tisha laughed.

Syd laughed too and tossed a pillow at her. She really loved spending time with Tisha. She was so down to earth and easy to talk to. "You really had me going. What do you want to watch?"

"Um, I don't know. Start scrolling. I'm sure something will catch our attention." She lay down on the couch so she could put her legs across Syd's lap. This wasn't anything new for them. She invaded Syd's personal space every time they were together. Syd certainly didn't mind. After flipping through comedies, sci-fi and horror, they couldn't agree on a movie, so they decided to switch to *Living Single* on Hulu.

When they got to the episode when Khadijah and Scooter took their friendship to the next level, the energy in the room shifted. They both felt it, but neither spoke about it. They made eye contact for a second and went back to watching the show. Syd repositioned herself on the couch, and Tisha's legs shifted but remained across Syd's lap. Syd really wanted to kiss her, but she knew she needed to respect the boundaries Tisha had set. She could no longer concentrate on the show. Syd needed to clear her head for a few minutes because there was nothing "friend zone" about her thoughts.

"I'm about to go to the kitchen and get something to drink. You want anything?" Tisha moved her feet off of Syd's lap and sat up. She was feeling something that she hadn't felt before. It was awkward, but in a good way. She wanted to tell Syd, but she was afraid.

"Uh, I could use a snack. Do you have any popcorn left?" she asked without making eye contact. Tisha really wanted to kiss Syd, but what if it made things weird or awkward between them afterwards? She had told Syd she didn't want a sexual relationship, but at this moment, Tisha wanted to retract everything she had said a few months ago. How did she go from watching TV to being trapped in her thoughts?

"I think so. I'll go check." When Syd made it to the kitchen, she exhaled without realizing beforehand that she had been holding her breath. She grabbed a bag of popcorn out of the cabinet and slapped it in the microwave.

"That *damn* Scooter! I forgot he kissed Khadijah. Now I'm feeling some type of way. I know she is, too. I can see it in her eyes," Syd mumbled while she watched the popcorn bag expand.

Tisha had grown anxious sitting on the couch. It had only been a minute, but it seemed like so much longer. She got up and went into the kitchen. Syd was resting her elbows on the counter, with her head in her hands.

"You okay in here?"

Startled, Syd jumped and looked Tisha in her eyes. She tried to detect whether there was something between them. Little did she know, Tisha was wondering the same thing. The microwave went off, but they continued to stare at each other for a few more seconds in silent tension. Since Syd didn't say anything, Tisha broke the stare-off and walked over to the microwave to get the bag of popcorn. She shook the bag a few times before she opened it. After she popped a few pieces of popcorn in her mouth, she stared into Syd's eyes. She swallowed the popcorn with a gulp and spoke up.

"Is it me, or is something weird going on between us right now?" Tisha asked.

"I feel it too," Syd replied quietly.

Tisha popped some more popcorn in her mouth and licked her fingers. They continued to stare at each other in silence.

"Fuck it," Sydney mumbled, rushing over to Tisha and kissing her on the lips. Tisha dropped the bag of popcorn and put her hands on Syd's face, returning the kiss. Syd smiled and grabbed Tisha's waist. Her hands lingered for a second, then she pulled her close. The softness of Tisha's lips made her shudder. They smiled at each other, then Syd frantically pulled down Tisha's tights, revealing that she wasn't wearing any panties. Syd picked Tisha up and sat her on the edge of the counter. She spread Tisha's legs apart and slowly inserted two fingers inside of her.

"Ahh!" Tisha moaned loudly as she put her hands on top of Syd's head. Syd loved when a woman rubbed or grabbed her head during sex. It was the ultimate turn on. Syd swirled in Tisha's juices until it dripped from her fingers. Playing with Tisha's pussy made Syd want to taste it. She eased her tongue inside Tisha's box and let Tisha's juices moisten her face. Three months after their "just friends" talk, things were suddenly and unexpectedly heating up between them.

It was Syd's chance for a friends-to-lovers situation, and she didn't regret it for one minute. From the moment Tisha decided to give in to her sexual urges—give in to Syd—their chemistry was undeniable. Everything about Tisha turned Syd on. From the way Tisha's eyes gleamed when she met Syd's gaze, to her touch, her lips…everything. If there was such a thing as perfection, Tisha was that.

"What are you daydreaming about?" Tisha asked, snapping Syd out of her thoughts.

Syd smiled. "I'm reminiscing about us and how we both said we only wanted to be friends, but here we are today in a relationship." They sat comfortably on the couch, Tisha's legs stretched across Syd's lap, as usual.

Tisha smiled back at her. "Yeah, somehow I let you con me," she said, giggling.

"Oh, is that right?" Syd replied then started tickling her feet.

"Baby! Stop it!" Tisha squealed as she tried to squirm away from her. Syd gently cuffed one of Tisha's heels so she could massage her foot. She hadn't cared for feet until she met Tisha. Tisha's feet were so soft, and her freshly painted toes were enticing. She started kissing them and then slowly opened her mouth so she could suck on Tisha's big toe. Tisha moaned and placed her hands on top of Syd's freshly faded head. Syd removed Tisha's toe from her mouth so she could make her way to Tisha's panties; she felt like doing some teasing tonight. She rubbed Tisha's pussy; her pussy lips looked like they were going to bust through her panties. Instead of pulling them off, Syd pulled them to the side to suck on Tisha's clit. Tisha moaned and rubbed the top of Syd's head some more. After several minutes of pleasing Tisha, Syd stopped sucking on Tisha's clit and stood up.

"I think the bed is calling our names," Syd declared with a smirk.

"Oh, yeah? Well, I think we should answer it," Tisha replied smartly.

Syd grabbed her hand and led her into the bedroom. Hopping on the bed, Tisha pulled off her top and her damp panties. She spread her legs apart and slowly stroked her clit while Syd watched. Tisha rubbed her wet pussy and slid her hands to her breasts to tug on her perfect nipples. Syd bit her lip as she watched with lustful eyes.

"Are you going to stand there and watch me, or are you going to come ride my pussy?" Tisha asked. Syd smiled and slowly removed her clothes. Tisha had been the first woman to ever grind her pussy on Syd. Before Tisha, Syd had used a strap, fingers or her tongue, but the first time Tisha put her pussy on top of Syd's and started riding Syd's bone, Syd came right away. Pussy grinding was an art, and Tisha had mastered it. She was on her knees and crawled to the edge of the bed, where Syd was standing. She took her left hand and ran it up and down Syd's stomach, looking into her eyes.

"Lie down now," she commanded. Syd loved when Tisha was dominant. She did as she was told so Tisha could straddle her. Tisha positioned herself so her left leg was in between Syd's legs. She put her pussy on top of Syd's and leaned forward so she could slide her tongue inside Syd's mouth. Syd squeezed and slapped Tisha's ass as they kissed. When they stopped kissing, Tisha clasped the side of Syd's throat with her right hand. She squeezed Syd's neck gently as she rode her pussy. Syd had a rush of adrenaline every time Tisha choked her during sex. She gripped Tisha's waist while she rode her vigorously.

"Mmm! Yes, baby! I love feeling your juicy pussy up against mine. Mmm!" Syd moaned and slapped Tisha's ass again. Tisha put her arm underneath Syd's left leg and continued to ride her. Syd bit her bottom lip and closed her eyes. After a few more strokes, Tisha let go of Syd's leg and gave her a kiss on the forehead.

"You know what I was just thinking about? It's been a long time since I've tasted you," Tisha said while she slowly descended to Syd's pussy. Once her mouth was right in front of it, she looked up at Syd hungrily and spread her legs apart. Syd placed a hand on Tisha's head and massaged her scalp as soon as she felt the tip of Tisha's tongue swipe up and down her clit.

"Ooh, baby, you're so wet," Tisha moaned. She sucked Syd's clit as Syd purred quietly. Her body shook and juices trickled down as Tisha sped up her tongue stroke.

"Oh, my God! Baby! I fucking love you!" Syd yelled, no longer able to keep her composure. She couldn't remember the last time Tisha had given her head. She knew it was partly her fault that Tisha hadn't done it in a while. Most of the time when they had sex, Syd would damn near eat Tisha into a coma, so she couldn't do much afterwards. Tisha was damn sure making up for lost time. She slid her thumb inside of Syd and continued to suck on her clit. Syd moaned loudly and inched back, scrambling to get away from the intense pleasure. Tisha giggled and stopped eating Syd's pussy to give her a quick kiss on the lips.

"I'm hungry. How about we go grab something to eat and then come back and have another round?" she asked, getting out of the bed.

"Of course, baby."

They threw on some clothes and rushed out the door. A good meal followed by more sex sounded like a perfect night.

TIA

Feenin'

Tia smiled, licked her lips slowly and inhaled deeply. She was still in the moment where she and Raquel had made sweet love. She wanted more of her—a lot more of her. She was sure Raquel had cast a spell over her body and soul. Their chemistry was so overpowering that sometimes it was scary. Unable to shake the feeling, Tia inhaled again to soak up the essence Raquel's sweet pussy left behind on her lips and on her fingers. All Raquel had to do was stare into her eyes and Tia would practically melt. The way she craved her was surely an addiction, and she didn't give a damn who knew. She *needed* some more of her, but Raquel had to go to work. She had a habit of making Raquel late, so she decided not to be greedy this morning. Even though their sex life was incredible, it was Raquel's mind that had Tia in awe.

They had first met at a poetry slam. Raquel had caught Tia's eye as soon as she stepped through the door—literally. Raquel was a member of a sorority, and she and two of her sorors had come into the building doing their thing. Tia noticed Raquel first because of her massive afro. While everything else seemed to be in place, her fro was wild and lush. It swayed every time she took a step. Her body language screamed confidence, and that really intrigued Tia. She didn't know if Raquel was a lesbian or not, but she wanted to get to know her, even if it was only as a friend.

"Alright, Thetas! I see you ladies came in here showing out. Don't they look lovely, everyone? I hope you all are enjoying yourselves tonight. I'm Amelia, your hostess this evening. As you can see, we have a few artists here showcasing their work. Show them some love by purchasing a piece of artwork. If you can't make a purchase today, take a business card and follow them on social media. I see a lot of you have already made your way to the bar; make sure you drink responsibly. If you don't have a boo or a friend to give you a ride home, we will gladly order you a Lyft so you won't be tempted to drive home drunk. We want everyone to make it back to your destination safely. If you're hungry, there are food trucks outside, so go ahead and grab you something to eat once we take a break. We have poets from all over coming up to spit some words. First up, we have my girl, Tia. Come on up here, Tia."

Tia loved getting in front of crowds and pouring out her heart. She hopped on stage smiling widely, dapping Amelia up before taking the mic from her.

*Oooh, look at that mahogany skin and
voluminous hair.
And those eyes—they are so mysterious.
I peered into them as if I could read into her soul.
I inhaled her air.
I say her air because she commanded the room
and demanded my attention.
She instructed me to see her, and indeed I did.
I saw her, but I want to know her.
I want to make love to her mind and tongue
kiss her soul.
I'm only human, but that doesn't mean I can't
be her superwoman.
I'll be her shoulder to lean on,
the person to rely on when she's feeling off
balance.
Loving her will not be a challenge because I'm
willing to learn who she is,
inside and out.
And this isn't some empty rhyme or a lame
pick up line.
It's nothing but the truth.
She's a beautiful Black queen, and if no one
has let her know,
I'm doing so tonight.*

Tia smiled and put the mic back on the stand. Amelia walked back on stage and picked up the mic.

"Now that was hot! It sounded like Tia might have been talking to one of you beautiful ladies out in the crowd," she announced, looking at Tia and smiling. She knew her friend well and couldn't wait to find out who she was crushing on. While the next poet was on stage, she pulled Tia to the side.

"Alright. So, who is she?"

Tia grinned slyly and playfully nudged Amelia's shoulder. "I knew you weren't going to wait until this event was over to ask me that. Just like you, I was eyeing the Thetas when they stepped in. Shorty with the afro is breathtaking. I've never seen her before, and she's very noticeable. Do you know who she is?"

"As a matter of fact, I do," Amelia replied with a smug grin on her face. "Her name is Raquel. She's single *and* she's a lesbian. That's all I really know about her."

"That's *all* you know? That's more than enough." Tia smiled, staring over at an unsuspecting Raquel. "Cool. Now that I know she's a lesbian, I can go introduce myself and see if we can get acquainted." Tia rubbed her hands together as though she'd just won a victory then chucked up the deuces to Amelia.

She scanned the room and spotted Raquel walking out of the restroom. "Perfect timing," she said to herself.

Wearing a warm smile, Tia walked up to Raquel as confident as a peacock. She had been called cocky a few times in her life, but in Tia's opinion, she was too humble to be cocky.

Once they were standing in the same space, Tia extended

her hand to Raquel. "Hello, I'm Tia," she greeted. "My friend told me you were new on campus. I was wondering if I could take you out to lunch sometime or maybe even to see a movie."

Raquel hesitated for a few seconds but then returned the gesture, with a quirky smile on her face. "Are you looking for a friend, fuck buddy or girlfriend?" she asked directly.

Tia bucked her eyes, surprised by the question. "You're very blunt," she noted. "I like that. I'm blunt too."

Raquel cleared her throat. "Yeah…I like to ask questions so I'm not confused later on down the line. Women have the bad habit of being fickle sometimes."

On those words, Tia decided to tread carefully. "Yeah, I completely understand where you're coming from, because I have run into quite a few that had me lost. But let me clear something up. I'm single, but I'm not looking for a fuck buddy. I also believe that before you can have a great relationship, you need to establish a friendship first."

Raquel nodded in approval, but Tia could tell she was unsure of how genuine she was. It didn't bother Tia too much. Raquel had every right to be skeptical since they were just getting to know each other.

"I'll take a lunch date, depending on where you're trying to take me," Raquel said with an eyebrow slightly raised.

"How about I surprise you? I'll let you know now that I'm vegetarian, so it won't be fast food."

"Cool. I'm vegan. It looks like you might have yourself a date."

Tia smiled. "Awesome. Are you leaving now?" Raquel nodded her response, and Tia followed with, "Okay, I'll walk you to your car."

When they made it to her car, Raquel didn't leave right away. She liked Tia's energy, so they stood in the parking lot talking. Tia really could have chatted with her all night. After about thirty minutes, they finally exchanged numbers and went their separate ways.

Tia waited patiently for Raquel to show up for their date. She wondered if maybe she had missed something during the week when they had been texting back and forth. Their conversations revealed that Raquel was apprehensive about getting close to anyone. Tia was unbothered, however. She felt she could change that by simply being herself. Tia felt that if something was meant for her, she should go for it, so she was glad that she and Raquel were finally meeting up. Or at least she hoped they still had a date. She had been waiting for Raquel for quite some time now. She had offered to pick her up, but Raquel politely declined.

Tia was positioned so she would be able to see Raquel as soon as she walked through the door. She pulled her phone out to check the time again. She wanted to text Raquel, but she didn't want to seem too pushy. When she looked up again, she locked eyes with Raquel as she strolled through the door. Just like the night they met, Raquel's body language commanded attention. There was so much poise and grace in her walk. She was wearing a little black dress with a pair of silver heels. Tia smiled, thinking Raquel already matched her fly; Tia was wearing a little black dress as well. She stood up so she could give Raquel a hug. "Nice to see you again, Raquel."

"Likewise. You clean up rather well," Raquel told Tia with a slick smile on her face.

"Yeah, I figured I'd dress up since this is a special occasion."

"Oh, it is?" Raquel questioned with laughter in her tone.

"I believe so. You can learn so much more about a person during face-to-face conversations. You can't read body language via text."

"You're right about that," Raquel replied, "and I'm going to keep it real with you. I declined your offer to pick me up because, even though you seem cool, if the date goes south, I want to be able to leave on my own accord."

Tia gave her a warm smile before replying. "Hey, I appreciate you keeping it real with me. I'll do the same."

They had a great date and ended up staying at the restaurant, chatting until it closed. Tia was pleased with how well it went. They agreed they could stand seeing each other on a regular basis, so they started spending time together frequently. Raquel was really passionate about astrology and anatomy. She introduced Tia to a world she knew nothing about: crystals, aligning chakras, and burning sage. It was all so intriguing. The first time Raquel invited Tia to her spot, they had a yoga session. Tia had never been around anyone like Raquel. She really enjoyed spending time with her.

"Um. I think I like you," Raquel said with a smile on her face.

Tia raised an eyebrow. "Just *think,* huh?"

"Well, I *know* I like you," Raquel corrected.

"Good, because I like you, too," Tia shared, taking Raquel's hand to kiss it. Tia really felt she loved Raquel. That notion seemed crazy since they hadn't even kissed yet. She stared into Raquel's acorn-colored eyes for a few seconds. This was the perfect moment to find out if her lips were as soft as they looked. Tia put her forehead against Raquel's and wrapped her arms around her in a tight embrace. Raquel bit her bottom lip and then kissed Tia tenderly. They had crossed the boundaries of the friend zone, but Tia decided to take things slowly. She left the kiss as just a kiss and didn't try to have sex with Raquel that day.

When they finally talked about having sex, Raquel didn't hold back. She came over to Tia's place with a bag full of sex toys. She let herself in and found Tia sprawled out on the bed. Raquel dangled the bag over Tia's face.

"I brought my bag of tricks to see if you can handle a woman of my caliber," she teased with a devilish grin.

"Aw, snap! I dunno; I'm feeling a lil' scared," Tia sputtered, laughing nervously. She had never dated anyone who used sex toys, so she didn't know what to expect. Raquel pulled out a vibrator with a cord attached.

"Wait. You're about to plug that in the wall and then stick that in my pussy?" Tia asked wide-eyed.

"It's not going inside you, only up against your clit. Trust me. You'll enjoy it. Take your clothes off."

Tia trusted Raquel; she got undressed and lay down on her back. Raquel smiled and turned on the vibrator. She waved it around with a seductive grin. "This is called a wand. It has three different speeds. I'll start on the lowest setting because it's very powerful."

She turned the wand on and pressed it against Tia's clit.

"Gah damn!" Tia yelped, clenching the sheets. If this was the lowest setting, she knew she wouldn't be able to handle the highest one. The pleasure was so intense Tia didn't know if she should moan or scream. "Oh my God, babe! This feels so fucking good! Ooh, shit! I'm about to come!" This was the first time she orgasmed so hard her toes curled. She was stunned.

Raquel kept the wand pressed up against her clit. She was getting off by watching Tia squirm around. The amount of pleasure was so intense that Tia couldn't take anymore.

"Fuck! Okay! I can't. Stop, baby," Tia moaned, inching away from Raquel. Raquel had a look of satisfaction on her face as she removed the wand from Tia's clit. She tossed it on the bed and then climbed on top of Tia and planted a kiss on her forehead. "Are you all tapped out, or can I pull out another toy? I got a new one just yesterday."

Tia was curious to know what else Raquel had up her

sleeve. She was also turned on by her directness. "I'm sure I can handle some more. What do you have in store for me?"

"I'll show you as soon as I get undressed. This toy is for both of us." Raquel smirked and pulled her shirt off. She wasn't wearing a bra, as usual. Even though it was their first time having sex, it wasn't the first time Tia had seen Raquel's breasts. Raquel didn't have a problem being a tease by getting naked in front of her. Tia didn't mind, though. Raquel had an exquisite body. She no longer had to daydream about making love to Raquel because it was about to become a reality.

Raquel pulled her sweats off and exposed her freshly shaved pussy. She reached into her bag and pulled out a long, pitch-black dong with two heads.

"Have you ever seen one of these?" Raquel asked, waving it lustfully at Tia.

"Um, not in real life." Tia had an eyebrow raised. She was both intrigued and nervous. Whenever she had sex, she always used her fingers.

"Don't worry, love. I'll be gentle…at first," Raquel warned with a mischievous grin.

Raquel had first been introduced to a double-sided dong by a woman she used to date. It took a certain level of finesse to use one because sometimes the dong could slip out. Raquel moistened both ends of the dong with her mouth.

"Spread your legs, and relax your body," she directed. Tia spread her legs apart slowly. Raquel gripped Tia's waist and eased one end inside of Tia. She then inserted the other end inside herself.

"Once you get the hang of using this, you'll love it," she whispered to Tia as she thrust forward. She gently held on to the middle of the dong so it would stay in place better. Tia was enjoying the pleasure she was feeling. She wrapped her legs around Raquel's waist. "You like that, baby?" Raquel whispered.

"Ooh, yes! This feels so good," Tia said in a low moan. The way Tia stared into Raquel's eyes turned her on even more. She came hard and then took the dong out of her pussy but continued to fuck Tia with it. Tia had come oozing out of her body—the dong was covered in it. Raquel kept sliding it in and out.

"Damn, girl! I love the way this feels!" Tia yelled and dug her nails into Raquel's back. Raquel smiled and sped up her pace a bit. "Ooh, baby...I can't take any more," she moaned. Raquel threw the dong on the bed and climbed on top of Tia. Tia let out a relaxing sigh as their pussies connected. "Fuck, girl! I don't know how you plan on topping that," Tia laughed.

Raquel put her mouth against Tia's ear. "Stick with me, and I'll show you."

Tia shuddered. "You damn right. I'm not going anywhere."

SHAN
Going to Hell

It had been a long time since Shan had attended a church service in her hometown. She was sure that nothing had changed. Once she made it to the parking lot, she sat in her car for a few minutes.

"Why am I here?" she mumbled before walking inside. She wanted to get to her seat unnoticed, but since her grandmother was seated in the front pew, she had to walk past all the disapproving stares. The church members were downright disrespectful. They were gawking at Shan like she was some kind of circus freak. She didn't know if they were looking in disapproval because they knew she was a lesbian or if it was because of how she dressed. She came to the church because she was asked, but she wasn't about to be uncomfortable by wearing women's clothing. The last time she was there, she had her long hair pulled back into a ponytail and wore a blouse with slacks because she didn't want people staring. Now, she dressed for herself and not for the world everywhere she went. Her hair was faded, and this time she had on a collared shirt and jeans. She was very comfortable, but the way they glared at her made her feel uncomfortable and out of place.

The only reason she was there in the first place was because her grandmother had been begging her to come. She accepted Shan for who she was, but the rest of the congregation most likely wanted to throw some holy water on her. She wanted to stop mid-stride and turn around and walk right back to her car. Even though she hadn't told her grandmother she was coming, she knew the members would make sure to let her know Shan had bolted out of the church. Shan knew that would hurt her grandmother's feelings, so she decided to ignore the stares and plopped down next to her grandmother. Grandma was so in tune with what the pastor was saying, Shan had to tap her on the shoulder to get her attention. She gasped with joy when she realized it was Shan.

"Would you look at God?" she whispered to Shan then kissed her on the cheek. "I'm so glad you came. We have a special program for Pastor Williams and the first lady. It's their anniversary today, so we have two services."

Ugh! Shan didn't reply; she only smiled and hugged her grandmother. Today was definitely the wrong Sunday to pop up. She wasn't trying to spend all day in church. One service was long enough, so there's no telling how long they would be there now since there were two. She scanned the church to see if there were any non-judgmental members present and locked eyes with Katrina.

Katrina was Pastor Williams' oldest daughter. Shan hadn't seen her in years, but she still looked the same. Shan had always wanted to be more than a friend to Katrina, but Katrina cared too much about what people would say about the preacher having a lesbian for a daughter. Katrina cared for Shan but had to suppress her urges in order to keep up the image her father had of her. Even though Shan understood why Katrina didn't want to come out, she had hoped she would one day change her mind.

For a moment, they stared into each other's eyes as if there was no one in the room but them. Katrina had a slight smile on her face. Shan wondered if she had been watching her since she walked inside.

Since the age of twelve, Shan knew she was a lesbian. Her twin sister was boy crazy and thought the world of them, but the only thing Shan liked about boys was the clothes they wore. At thirteen, she told her parents she felt like she had been born into the wrong body. She didn't want to be a boy but felt as if she was built like one. She had very broad shoulders, a flat chest and no curves at all. Her mother told her not to worry and told her she was a late bloomer— God was only taking his time with her. Shan had wanted to tell her mother that she wasn't worried because she *liked* looking like a boy, but she kept quiet.

Once Shan hit puberty, nothing changed, so she started wearing men's clothing. Her mother tried to object by telling her she would only buy Shan the clothes she wanted her to wear. Shan wasn't bothered. She got a part-time job so she could buy her own clothes. At that time, her mother's main concern was what others would say. She didn't want anyone to see Shan dressed like a boy. She was ashamed, but mostly confused. She couldn't understand why Shan wanted to dress that way. By the time Shan graduated from high school, her mother had come around and accepted her daughter for who she was. She was a lesbian, but most importantly, she was her child, and at the end of the day, that's what really mattered.

Shan wasn't the least bit interested in the sermon. She'd been daydreaming the whole service and hadn't listened to one word. She hoped it would be over soon so she could catch up with Katrina. She glanced over at her again. Katrina did not meet her gaze this time. She appeared to be listening intently to her father's preaching. Shan excused herself and went to the restroom. She really wanted to walk past the restroom and out the front doors. She wasn't welcome there, so faking it was kind of draining her. On her way to the restroom, Shan felt eyes on her. She even saw a woman shake her head with disapproval. She was sure there was someone else in the congregation who wished they had the gall to be themselves instead of who the church said they needed to be. Too many people worried about upholding images that appease others, and for what?

Shan had been sitting in the restroom for about five minutes. She knew she needed to get back, but she was really reluctant to do so. As soon as she stepped out of the stall, Katrina was walking through the door.

"I figured you were in here hiding," she said with a chuckle.

Shan smiled. She wanted to extend her arms for a hug, but it had been so long since they had hugged each other. She wasn't sure if Katrina would welcome it or not.

"Just like when we were kids. I couldn't wait until service was over, so I'd come in here and hide until my grandmother came in and got me. I see your pops is still long-winded." They laughed in unison.

Shan stared into her eyes. Katrina was so beautiful. Her butterscotch skin seemed to glow. It had been years since they had seen each other, but now that Shan was back in town for a while, she hoped they could see more of each other, even though Katrina had broken her heart. Shan walked over to the sink and started washing her hands. Katrina waited for her to turn the water off before saying what was on her mind.

"It's been a long time, Shan…about five years, right? I thought about you a lot while you were gone. I would check your Facebook page from time to time to try to take a peek into your life. I really missed you."

Shan frowned and rolled her eyes. "Really, Trina? We said we would stay in touch, but after six months, you stopped responding to my calls and text messages. I didn't think you would switch up on me like that. We've known each other since before we could walk. I loved you. As a matter of fact, I still love you. I was so hung up on what we never had that I couldn't get into a serious relationship with anyone. Shit's wild."

Katrina put her head down and shuffled her feet. When she looked up, she had tears in her eyes. "I'm sorry, Shan. I was slightly jealous. Well, more than slightly. You had made the decision to leave, and I decided to stay so I wouldn't disappoint my father. I chose his faith over love, and I have regretted that decision every day. I dated Deacon Shaw's son, Patrick, for a while. Two gay people trying to pretend we were straight. Time seemed to fly by and before I knew it, we had been together for two years. We lived the lie for so long, we had even started to believe we were a real couple. He proposed to me at a church picnic. We had them all fooled at the cost of our own happiness." Katrina paused.

"Everyone started asking us when we were going to get married and start having babies," Katrina continued. "We told them we wanted to wait until after medical school. We moved in together shortly after he proposed but had separate rooms. He would bring men back to the house, and I would have women over. Neither one of us committed to having serious relationships with the people we brought over. We were just hooking up with them. We were close to the three-year mark when he met James. There's no telling how long it would have gone on if it hadn't been for him. James, by far, was the most beautiful man I had ever laid eyes on. He wasn't flamboyant; he was just naturally beautiful. Anyway, we were having dinner at Tabitha's when James walked in. Patrick was practically drooling when he saw him. They locked eyes for a moment and then James went to the counter to pick up his call-in order. I remember putting my hand on top of Patrick's and whispering, 'Go talk to him.'"

"Are you sure I should? What if he's taken?"

"The way you two locked eyes, I think you could have a chance at love for real. I know we can't keep this charade up forever. We shouldn't have kept it up for this long. Now, go! Catch him before he leaves."

"Patrick gave me a quick peck on the cheek and nervously walked towards James. While they were talking, James looked over at me and I waved and smiled. Six months later, Patrick came out to his parents. He was so scared. He had to come out, otherwise James was going to stop dating him. James had told him he was tired of hiding in the shadows. Of course, Deacon Shaw wasn't happy when Patrick broke the news. He told James he wasn't welcome in their home or at church. Of course, Patrick was hurt, but he wasn't going to stop dating James. They ended up moving to Atlanta a few months after he came out. To this day, they're still together, and I'm so happy for them. Deacon Shaw didn't want my father or the other members of the church to know his son was gay, so he asked me if I could tell them we broke off our engagement because I didn't want to have children. I told him I wasn't about to keep lying, so I told my father the truth. I didn't tell him about Patrick, but I did tell him I'm a lesbian. I thought he would disown me, but to my surprise, he told me he loved me and I should do what makes me happy. I spent so many years afraid he would reject me…I put my happiness on hold out of fear. I wanted to reach out to you and tell you I was finally living my truth, but I was scared of rejection. When I saw you come in this morning, I told myself I was going to make sure you didn't leave without me telling you how I feel."

Shan forgot they were in the church restroom and grabbed Katrina's hands. She kissed them and then pulled Katrina into an embrace and kissed the top of her head. She held Katrina tightly and rubbed her back. She smelled so good. It had been too long since Shan had breathed her in, so long since they had embraced. Shan wanted more than an embrace, though. She stepped back and looked Katrina in her eyes. Katrina smiled, so Shan kissed her softly on the lips. Then she kissed Katrina's neck, and before they knew it, they were in one of the restroom stalls kissing. Shan had always envisioned their first time. It surely wasn't in a church. But they were so caught up in the moment that neither one of them cared. Shan got on her knees and eased her hands up Katrina's skirt. She started to remove Katrina's pantyhose but stopped abruptly.

"What's wrong?" Katrina asked in a hoarse whisper.

"Are you sure you want to do this *here*? You mean so much more to me than a church restroom hookup."

Katrina smiled devilishly and put her hands on Shan's head. "I know I do, so make sure you fuck me real good."

That reassurance was all Shan needed to hear. She slowly ran her hands up Katrina's legs again and pulled her pantyhose off. Once she removed the pantyhose, she pulled

Katrina's panties down. Shan no longer had to fantasize about Katrina's love nest now that it was in her face. She gave it a kiss and then started rubbing her clit. Katrina moaned quietly and then threw her leg over Shan's shoulder to give her easier access. Shan gently slid her thumb inside and started moving it in and out while continuing to rub on Katrina's clit with her forefinger.

"Ooh, yes!" Katrina shouted, forgetting she was in the church restroom.

That drove Shan wild, so she moved her thumb in and out faster. Katrina put both her hands on top of Shan's head and continued to moan. Shan hadn't even stuck her tongue in yet, but Katrina was already going crazy.

"Oh, my God! What kind of devilish work is going on here? This is the Lord's house, you heathens!" Sister Patterson yelled as she banged on the stall door.

Neither Shan nor Katrina mumbled a word. There was really nothing they could say since they had obviously been caught. Shan picked up Katrina's panties off the floor and stuffed them in her pocket while Katrina struggled to put her stockings back on.

"Come on out of there! I want to see your faces! I could hear you moaning as soon as I walked in the door. You should be ashamed. Damn nasty devils!"

Shan unlocked the stall door, and out waltzed her and Katrina. Neither of them had any kind of remorse, but both were upset that the moment had been ruined. Sister Patterson gasped and clutched her chest once she realized

Katrina was one of the people in the stall. They stood there for a few seconds in awkward silence because no one really knew what to say. Sister Patterson was shocked that Pastor's daughter was having some type of sexual relations in the restroom, and with a girl-boy at that. She was more than ready to embarrass the culprits until she found out it was Katrina. She expected Shan to do something so unholy, but not the beloved Katrina.

"Well, you know it would crush your father's heart if I embarrassed you in front of the entire church. That's the only reason I'm not going to go back out there and say anything to the congregation. You two really need to seek Jesus and ask for forgiveness." She still had her hands on her chest.

"Sister Patterson, no disrespect, but if you ever feel the need to try to embarrass anyone…you need to start with your husband," Katrina responded. Katrina's response shocked the elderly church member, but she had no words. She went into one of the stalls and slammed the door. Katrina and Shan snickered like children.

"Come on. Let's get out of here," Katrina commanded, grabbing Shan by the hand. They rushed out of the front doors of the church. "Where'd you park?" she asked excitedly.

"I parked towards the back. Where are we going? You're leaving your car here?" Shan asked, curious to know what Katrina's plan was.

"Yeah, I'm leaving my car. We're going back to my place

so I can ride your face like I should have done a million years ago. We have to make up for lost time."

With that, Shan happily escorted Katrina to her car. Her church visit had turned out way better than she had expected.

JADE

Cake

Jade angrily kicked her covers to the floor. She'd been tossing and turning all night, so she had finally given up on drifting off to sleep. It wasn't happening because her mind was too busy. She knew she should have deleted Alex from her Snapchat months ago, but she couldn't seem to let her go. She watched all of her snaps faithfully, and now she regretted it. Alex was on vacation in Miami with some chick Jade had never seen before. She wondered how long they had known each other, because she and Alex had only been broken up for four months. That didn't seem to Jade like enough time to be moving on with someone else, but Alex clearly had a different mindset. She and the chick had even gotten matching palm tree tattoos. Really? A matching tattoo with some brand-new female! Jade grabbed her iPhone again to see if she had posted any more snaps. Once she watched them, she tossed her phone on the bed and buried her head in her hands.

She and Alex had made future plans, and now Alex was

living her best life without Jade. Even though their breakup wasn't bad, Jade's pain was. They broke up because Alex said she had become emotionally detached and needed her own place. Alex told Jade she still loved her, but love wasn't enough. They were still living together when Alex removed all the pictures that Jade had tagged her in on Facebook and then removed her as a friend. Jade, on the other hand, still had every picture she had posted of the two of them together. They shared some good memories, so it was hard for her to delete Alex from her life. They were friends before the relationship, and even though Alex had assured her that they would remain friends, Jade knew now she was only saying that to make her feel better. Some days she was fine with the loss of their relationship, but other days, it hurt her to her core. Today was undeniably one of those days.

Watching Alex's snaps really did a number on Jade's soul. She had hoped Alex would have a change of heart and come back with an apology, but she was cuddled up on the beach with her feet in the fucking sand. Ugh! Even though Jade was aware that she had been sulking about it entirely too much, she didn't know how to unglue her eyes from the screen. She crawled out of her bed and grabbed her notebook and a pen.

> *I watched my soul evaporate right before my*
> *eyes. It was within my grasp but outside of*
> *my control. I cried out, but my cries went*
> *unheard. They may have been heard, but*

*what I was crying for wasn't for me. I know
that to be true, but I cannot seem to repair
myself. Even as I write these words, I wonder
what was in the connection that won't let my
heart fully heal. I say that I'm over it one day,
and then the next, I'm reliving the images of
us together. I can't get them out of my head.
I want to erase the pain...I wish I could heal.*

What was she thinking? Writing down her feelings only made her feel worse. Maybe if she went out and had some fun, it would help take her mind off of things for a bit. Reece, an ex of hers, had invited Jade to hang out with her and her girlfriend a few weeks after her breakup. She declined because, at the time, she didn't feel like being social. She knew she would have a good time if she went, but she couldn't get out of the funk she was in. Reece was cool. She and Jade had dated five years prior to Jade dating Alex. Reece was six years younger than Jade, but she had shown Jade that age didn't mean shit when it came to sexual performance. Reece was a wonderful lover. They ended up being lovers longer than they were a couple, though, because once they decided to put a title on it, Reece realized she wasn't ready to commit. She ended up cheating on Jade with one of her exes. Their relationship fizzled after only a month, and Jade was pissed more than anything. They could have just remained friends with benefits instead of coupling up. Reece had wasted her time, so Jade cut off all ties with her. Two years later, Reece finally came to her with a genuine apology, so they resumed their friendship, with an occasional fuck every now and then.

"Fuck these tears!" Jade mumbled to herself angrily. All the crying in the world wouldn't bring Alex back into her life. She needed to get over her and move the fuck on. She wasn't looking to get into a relationship, but a good fuck would slow her thoughts for a bit. She decided to hit Reece up and see if she had any plans for the night.

Jade was standing between Reece and Justice. Justice was Reece's current girlfriend, and, ironically, she and Jade were already acquainted with one another. Justice knew that Reece and Jade had previously dated, but she didn't have a problem with Jade hanging out with them. Reece had convinced Jade to meet up with them at a local bar. Jade looked around the room at everyone. They all looked so cheerful, talking and laughing with each other, and Jade only wanted to drown her heartache in alcohol. She knew her pain would return once she was sober, but at least the alcohol would bring Jade temporary happiness.

"You look like you could use a drink," Justice told Jade, as if she had read her mind.

Jade forced a smile. "Yeah, I think a drink would help loosen me up a bit. It's been a while since I've been out, and there are a lot of people here."

Justice put her hand on Jade's shoulder. "I know something that will help loosen you up, but a drink will have to do for now."

She didn't wait for Jade to respond; she removed her hand and sashayed to the bar. Jade watched her walk away. Justice was wearing some jeans that looked like they were perfectly molded onto her frame. Her ass looked so good in them, Jade watched until Justice was no longer visible.

"You should see how good she looks when she's naked," Reece whispered in Jade's ear and then licked the bottom of her lobe. Jade shuddered and her pussy immediately started throbbing. If she needed a sign of what the couple's intentions were that night, they had both made it crystal clear. Shit, why not? Jade already knew Reece knew how to fuck her the way she liked, and after seeing Justice walk off, she wanted to rub all on her ass.

Three drinks and two hours later, Jade was sitting in the couple's living room smoking a blunt. She was super relaxed and had nothing but sex on her mind. Jade passed the blunt to Reece, who'd had about five drinks, so she was on a whole different level than Jade. Justice had gone to slip into something more comfortable and came back out wearing a sports bra and some boy shorts. Her caramel skin seemed to glow, and her thick thighs looked like they were begging to be rubbed down. Jade couldn't help but stare at Justice with her mouth open. She shifted in her seat and took a deep breath. It was like she just realized she was really about to sleep with her ex and her ex's new girlfriend. Justice took a seat between them, so Reece passed the blunt to her.

"You want a charge?" Justice asked Jade after she took a hit.

"Yeah, sure," Jade replied timidly. Her heart was racing. Could she really go through with this? Justice took a hit of the blunt and then passed it back to Reece. Reece got up and went to the kitchen. Justice inched closer to Jade and placed both of her hands on Jade's face. She blew the smoke she had been holding into Jade's mouth. After Jade inhaled and then exhaled, Justice kissed her. Her lips were so juicy. Jade placed a hand on the nape of Justice's neck and slid her tongue inside Justice's mouth. They were so in tune with one another, they didn't see Reece come up. Reece started kissing Jade on the back of her neck. Jade had chills running up and down her spine and her pussy was throbbing. She wondered if they could hear her heart pounding. She was ready for whatever was coming next.

"Take off your clothes," Justice directed in a sultry voice.

Jade was both nervous and excited as she obliged and stripped down to her birthday suit. Justice and Reece did the same. Once they were all undressed, Justice and Reece both started rubbing all over Jade's body. Jade was in heaven. She had four hands touching all over her and was sure she would climax from the rubbing alone. Justice cuffed her left titty and Reece had her right one. Both of them started licking and sucking on them at the same time. Jade threw her head back and smiled. She was enjoying the attention they were giving her body. Justice took it a step further and worked her way down to Jade's pussy with her tongue. She moved her tongue so swiftly, Jade came right away. Justice swallowed her juices and continued to swirl her tongue inside while Reece kissed Jade's titties. Jade gripped a handful of Reece's locs and threw her head back as her body shook. Justice got up from between Jade's legs and grabbed some of Reece's locs as well and tugged on them. Reece took the hint and made her way down to Jade's pussy. It was her turn to lick the juicy center. Justice cuffed Jade's chin and then slid her tongue into her mouth. While the two of them were kissing, she playfully pulled on Jade's nipples. Jade was enjoying every second. She had two women catering to her sexual needs, and it was *everything*. Justice abruptly stopped kissing her and got up and went into the bedroom.

"Should we follow her?" Jade asked Reece. She didn't know if there were any rules to threesomes or not. She wanted to kiss her, but since Justice had left the room without saying anything, she was unsure about what she should do next.

"No, she'll be back. She went to get my strap," Reece replied. She could tell Jade was still a little nervous, so she rubbed her thighs. Or maybe she wasn't nervous. She had a gleam in her eye. Maybe she was anxious to know what was going to happen next.

"Oooh, you strapping me down tonight?" Jade's eyes got

wide and she had a smirk on her face. Even though it had been a while, she could never forget how good her pussy felt when Reece was dicking her down with the thick, black dong. She wondered if she still had it or if she had gotten a new one. Reece kissed her on her neck before replying.

"I'm going to let Justice use it on you this time. She told me how she's been wanting to fuck you, so since we have the opportunity, I'm going to let her have fun with you."

"Well, I won't object to that at all," Jade replied.

Justice walked back into the living room wearing the strap. She was stroking the dong with her hand like it was a real dick. They all laughed in unison. Jade figured she was trying to lighten the mood a bit. She was no longer nervous, though, only curious. She had never had a feminine woman strap her before. She was eager to see if Justice knew what she was doing. Justice seemed to read her mind and strolled up to her. She pulled her to the edge of the couch and parted her legs. She licked her lips.

"I see you're already wet for me. Do you want it slow, or do you like it rough?" she asked while caressing Jade's thighs.

"Um, it's been a while, so I think I want it slow."

Justice bit down on her bottom lip. She gripped Jade's thighs and entered Jade's pussy slowly. Jade moaned loudly as the dong eased inside of her. She wrapped her legs around Justice's back and placed her hands on her shoulders. Justice started off slowly, but now she was making swift, deep strokes. Jade was loving every second of it. Reece fired up another blunt and watched the two of them until they somehow ended up on the floor.

"I want you on top," Justice whispered in Jade's ear. She climbed off of Jade and sat on the edge of the couch. Jade placed her hands on Justice's shoulders and straddled her. She gyrated on the dong, digging her nails into Justice's shoulders. Justice gripped her waist as she bounced her up and down. They both had their eyes closed, heads back, and lips slightly parted. They were fucking like estranged lovers who had reunited. Reece was enjoying being a voyeur and decided not to interrupt them. Instead, she slowly stroked her clit with her middle finger. Watching her ex-lover and her current lover intertwined like a pretzel, she had never been this turned on before. She moaned as she continued to caress her clit.

Justice heard her moaning and opened her eyes. She outstretched her arm in her direction. "Come over here and join us, baby."

"Hmm? Give me a second. I'm about to come." Reece stroked her clit faster and threw her head back. After she released, she strolled to the couch. Jade had stopped riding Justice so Justice could take the strap off. Justice took some pillows off the couch and threw them on the floor to lie down on them. Reece sat on Justice's face and Jade spread Justice's legs open so she could eat Justice's pussy. It was so fat and juicy; it tasted better than Jade had imagined. She drove her tongue as deep as it would go and whirled it around until Justice had saturated her face with her juices. Reece had reached her climax at the same time and climbed off of Justice's face. Reece grabbed Jade's shoulders and gently guided her to lie on her back. Then she started massaging Jade's legs. Reece bent down so she could lick Jade's thighs. While she was teasing Jade, Justice went around her so she could make her way to Jade's lips. They locked lips as Reece slid her tongue up and down Jade's clit.

Justice stopped kissing Jade and went to roll up another blunt. Reece continued to lick on Jade's clit. Jade moaned as Reece lifted her legs and rested them on her shoulders. She stopped licking her clit and eased two fingers inside her. Jade wrapped her legs around Reece's neck and squeezed.

"I know it feels good, but don't choke me to death," Reece joked.

"Ooh, my bad. I didn't even realize I was doing it," Jade apologized.

"Shit you can keep doing it...just loosen up some."

Justice returned with a lit blunt in her hand. She took a hit and then gave Jade a charge. They started kissing again, so Reece took the blunt out of Justice's hand. Reece took a few hits and tapped Justice on her shoulder so she could take it back. Justice took the blunt and walked away. Reece fingered Jade until she couldn't take anymore.

"Damn, what a night," Jade managed to mouth in the middle of panting. She was all fucked out and couldn't move from the floor.

ATARI & COLE

Skin

Cole was sick and tired of living in Virginia, so when her cousin Tasha suggested she move to Texas, she was elated. She would have a place to stay as well as employment opportunities. There was no reason to say no.

Tasha was right about Cole being able to find a job quickly. The living situation, however, turned out to be a complete and utter nightmare: no room of her own and sharing the space with six adults and four children—in a four-bedroom house! When Cole arrived, Tasha gave her a tour of the home and showed her the room she was sleeping in, which was also occupied by two adults and a teenager. Tasha apologized for forgetting to tell her that a few extra people had moved in the last time she called her.

Yeah, that's not something that would be easily forgotten, Cole thought to herself. Cole hadn't been in the house two minutes and was already annoyed. Her frustration ballooned when she saw the variety of cats and dogs running around. *Great. A house full of people and animals.*

Cole glanced into the kitchen and was completely mortified. The pile of dirty dishes in the sink looked like it had been there for days. Someone had also spilled something on the floor, and one of the dogs was trying to lick it up. Tasha saw the look on her cousin's face but didn't say anything about the mess. She only mentioned that the water had recently been shut off. She told Cole not to worry because at night, her fiancé would go outside with a pair of pliers and turn it back on. Cole was floored. She felt a wave of nausea coming on. She excused herself and went into the bathroom.

The bathroom was more disturbing than the kitchen. She plopped down on the toilet and put her face in her hands. After seeing these living conditions, she wanted to hop on the next flight back to Virginia. If Cole hadn't already spent most of her money getting there, she would have bought a plane ticket back immediately. This was not a good situation. She was so mad at her cousin for inviting her to live there, knowing full well the living conditions were below standard. She couldn't believe they were okay living like that. Everyone in the house walked around as if being filthy was normal.

For the next two weeks, Cole tried to work as much as possible so she wouldn't have to be in that disgusting house. When she received her first paycheck, she decided to get a hotel room for a few days, spending her time checking Craigslist to see if she could find anyone who was looking for a roommate. She had to get out of that house before she lost all of her sanity. After searching for a few days to no avail, she finally found a place in Houston that wasn't too far from her job. When she spoke to her potential roommate, Cole learned that she would have her own room and bathroom. Cole wasn't going to just take her word for it and make the same mistake twice.

She went and checked out the townhouse before agreeing to enter into a lease. She was very pleased at how neat and tidy everything was and was fortunate to be able to move in the same day. Her new roommate had a young child, but she quickly discovered they weren't at home most of the time, so she got to have the place to herself quite a lot.

After being in Houston for a little over a year, Cole started to get lonely. For the most part, she worked and went home. Every now and then, she would hang out with one of her coworkers, but more often, she did everything solo. She downloaded a dating app called Plenty of Fish to see if she could find some companionship. It was much easier for her to spark up a conversation online than it was in person. She could never outright walk up to a woman she found attractive. She was way too nervous to do that. She figured it would be easier online, but every single woman she was supposed to meet up with was either crazy or would flake on her. Texas women had her deeply confused. What was the point of telling someone you were going to meet up with them only to be a no-show? She'd rather they reject her off top, instead of pretending to be interested.

Cole was about to say fuck it and just be lonely, but she came across the profile of a woman who had recently moved to Houston. After Cole read her bio, she decided she would send her a message. It didn't take Atari long to respond, and after a few days of texting through the app, they exchanged numbers. Cole enjoyed conversing with Atari, and she felt like the feeling might be mutual. She wanted to ask Atari out on a date, but she was hesitant. She wondered if she should let Atari make the first move.

Things had been going smoothly for Atari until she lost her job of seven years; shortly after, she and her girlfriend parted ways. She was at a loss and had to think hard about what she should do with her life. It wasn't only herself that Atari had to support. She was the mother of four. She had spent the better portion of her adult life working to live and not doing the work she loved. It was time to change that.

Atari had always had a passion for cooking, so she decided to go to culinary art school. Atari had heard great things about the Art Institute, so after doing some research of her own, she went and visited the one in Houston. She took a tour and decided she would enroll, just in time for summer classes. The place where she lived was an hour and a half commute to the Art Institute, so she only went to campus three days a week. After the third week of school, Atari was able to land a part-time job in Houston. That meant she would be doing a lot more driving back and forth. She called her ex-husband and asked him if he could keep their three youngest children for a school year. Her oldest was eighteen, so Atari decided to let her stay at home. Her summer was spent driving back and forth until her best friend moved to Houston in August and told Atari she could move in with her.

By October, Atari made the decision to rent her house out because she didn't bring in enough money to pay the bills there and contribute to bills at her best friend's home. She asked her mother if her oldest could stay with her until she graduated from high school. Atari had never been away from her children for more than a summer, so she was depressed being in Houston without them. She told herself it was to attain a better life for all of them, so she pressed on.

Atari soon realized that all she did was work and go to school. She wanted to get out and meet new people but didn't know where to start. Her best friend told her to download the POF (Plenty of Fish) app. She had met a few nice people on there but also warned Atari that she might come across a lot of crazy people, too.

"Girl, make sure you're cautious about giving your number out, in case you have to block them once you realize they aren't wrapped too tight."

"I'll keep that in mind," Atari replied, waiting for the app to download. She made sure her profile said she was only interested in meeting friends. Once she started receiving messages, she instantly became annoyed. It seemed like most of the women who messaged her hadn't bothered reading her bio and were only looking to hook up. When she received the message from Cole, she scrolled to her page and read Cole's bio. Cole was only looking for friends too, so Atari messaged her back. She let Cole know off top that she had children and wouldn't have a lot of free time once they joined her in Houston. Cole told her she understood, so after communicating with each other for a few days, they decided to meet at the mall.

When Cole saw Atari in person, she was much taller than Cole had assumed. Even though she was wearing flats, she still towered over Cole. It was also Cole's first time seeing a woman with locs. She wanted to reach out and touch them, but she wasn't about to ask on their first meetup. That would be so awkward! Instead, they walked around the mall and talked about their day.

Atari thought Cole was cute, aside from her hair. Someone had braided it back for Cole, and it was unraveling. She told Atari it had only been up for three days before her curls decided to break free. Cole put on a cap to hide it, but took it off to show Atari.

"You know, if you and I are going to be hanging out, I can't let you be out here with me looking a mess," Atari told her bluntly. "Can I see if I can dread it up?"

Cole agreed, so Atari went to Cole's place to get her started on her loc journey. After two days, Atari still wasn't done, and that's because they spent most of their time chitchatting and smoking weed. Cole didn't mind, though; she liked spending time with Atari. She asked Atari out on a real date because the mall meetup didn't count. Atari told her she would love to and asked Cole to pick the place. Cole chose one of her favorite places, Vintropolis, a wine bar that wasn't too far from her job. It was never crowded, so it was the perfect place to have a date. They decided they would meet there the following day, once Atari got out of class.

Atari walked into Vintropolis and saw Cole sitting at the bar. She smiled and they exchanged hugs. She wasn't much of a wine drinker but decided it wouldn't hurt to try something new. Cole was an experienced wine drinker, so she ordered a wine she thought Atari would like as well as a tray of grapes and cheeses. Their date lasted a little over an hour, and they both really enjoyed each other's company. Cole had caught an Uber there, so Atari offered to drop her off at home. Once they arrived, Cole stepped out of Atari's car for a hug. Smiling and extending her arms, she wrapped them around Atari and slowly ran her hand down to the small of Atari's back.

Atari wanted to act nonchalant, but she had chills running through her body. *Friends...friends...all I need is friends,* Atari chanted in her head while they were locked in their embrace. She didn't want to go home. She wanted to pretend she was drunk so Cole would invite her up. She would shyly accept and tell Cole she only needed to lie down for a bit. She wasn't going to be upfront with her intentions.

What if Cole thought she was some kind of ho, though? No, she needed to get her hormones in check and leave her panties on. She had said she was only looking for friends; aside from that, if she wanted to hook up with anyone, she had an ex who lived in Beaumont and was more than willing to fulfill her sexual needs. *That hug, though.*

"Are you okay?" Cole asked, sounding concerned.

"Oh, I'm fine. The wine has me on another level, that's all."

"Do you need to come up for a little bit?"

"No, I'm being extra. I'm good to drive. I'll text you when I make it home."

"Great. It was nice hanging out with you."

"Same. I'll be back. After all, I do need to finish your hair."

When Atari made it home, she texted Cole to let her know she was safe and immediately hopped on Snapchat to talk about their date.

"Ooh, so I'm sure y'all saw my post of the wine I had earlier on my date. I ended up having two glasses. If I'd had one more, she would have gotten some pussy tonight! I can't even lie. That hug she gave me when I dropped her off has me curious. I think I'm going to fuck her."

Atari put her phone down and gathered up some clothes so she could hop in the shower. The glasses of wine had her feeling lovely. She grabbed her loofah and body wash and lathered her body up in the shower. She thought about Cole and the way Cole had hugged her; she was getting horny.

Atari rinsed off the soap and removed the detachable shower head, turning the water on full blast to let it beat up against her throbbing pussy. She propped a leg on the side of the tub so she could have easier access to her pussy. She started playing with herself, imagining what Cole would be like in bed. That hug was so simple, but it really did something to her. She moved her fingers in and out of her pussy while the water continued to beat against it.

"Hmm...yeah, since just the thought of her has my mind going, I know I need to fuck her," Atari said out loud.

Atari liked fingering herself, but she loved it when someone else was doing the satisfying for her. She turned the water off and climbed out of the shower. She hadn't had enough, so Atari decided to have another session with herself. Even though Atari could get off without watching porn, she pulled up a video of a lesbian couple she liked to watch. She could tell porn was more than a job for them, so Atari watched them often. She lay in bed on her stomach and slid two fingers inside of her pussy so she could ride them. After several minutes of self-satisfaction, Atari was able to make herself come.

Yeah. She was fucking Cole without a doubt.

After about a week of twisting Cole's hair, Atari was finally finished with it. "You know it's your fault it took me so long to finish this, right?" Atari asked her after she was done blow drying Cole's hair.

"Is that right?" Cole asked her with a slight laugh. Atari liked Cole's laugh and the way her eyes looked closed every time she did it. It was so cute. Atari walked over to Cole's bed and plopped down.

"Yep. Every time I come over here, we get super high and go to Waffle House," Atari joked.

"Well, I knew I would keep getting to see you since you had to come back anyway to finish my hair," Cole replied.

"I like spending time with you. Did you watch my snap after our date?"

"No, I didn't see it. I don't think I downloaded the app until the next day."

"Well, it was all about you."

"Oh, really? What'd you say?"

"I was talking about that hug you gave me. I can't lie; it had me curious about your sex game. I wasn't going to say anything, but I can't stop thinking about it. I want to have sex with you, but I need to ask you a very important question first." Atari raised an eyebrow and paused for dramatic effect.

"Okay. What's your question?"

"Are you crazy?"

Cole laughed before replying. "We're all a little crazy. I don't think I'm any crazier than the next person."

"Oh, okay. Well do you want to have sex?"

"Hell yeah," Cole blurted, sashaying over to Atari like a lioness about to pounce on her prey.

Both her hands roamed up Atari's legs as she made her way to her plump breasts. She wanted to rip Atari's clothes off, but she decided to take it easy. Cole let her hands roam back down to Atari's thighs. Atari didn't know if it was the weed that had her body tingling, or if it was the way Cole was undressing her with her eyes. Maybe it was a combination. All she knew for sure was that she was ready for whatever Cole was about to do to her.

"Do you want me to take off my clothes, or do you want to help me?" Atari asked. Cole licked her lips and smiled. Atari smiled back shyly at her but didn't wait for Cole to answer. She removed her shorts and then her panties, slowly and seductively tossing them to the floor and rubbing her thighs. Cole was enticed; she licked her lips and made her way to Atari's luscious body. Even though she hadn't tasted her yet, Cole could already tell she wouldn't be disappointed. She parted Atari's legs and kissed her inner thigh before she drove her tongue inside of her sticky center. Cole stopped after a couple of seconds and got up and went to her closet. She grabbed a shoe box from the top and pulled out a small vibrator. She opened a cleansing wipe and sanitized it before she made her way back to Atari. She turned the vibrator on and then pressed it up against the bottom of Atari's clit. Atari moaned and eased down further in the bed. Cole eased the vibrator inside of her and started licking Atari's clit. Atari's moans were really turning her on. She turned the vibrator off and slid her tongue inside of Atari's wet pussy. After a couple of minutes, her face was saturated with Atari's juices. She stopped, licked her lips and continued to eat Atari's pussy.

"*Yes!*" Atari moaned, clenching the sheets. She had figured it would be good, but Cole exceeded her expectations.

Living Room Flow

"Bitch, guess what?" Terrance asked excitedly as soon as Aianna answered her phone. Terrance and Aianna had been friends since middle school, and whenever he had news to share, she was the first person he called.

"Don't keep me waiting in suspense. What is it?" Aianna never tried to guess what he had to tell her because it could really be anything, coming from him.

"Ugh! You never like to guess! One day you're going to play along. Anyway, I just found out that Slutty Vegan is in town for one day only. They're set up downtown from three to nine. I know you were sad we didn't get to go when we visited ATL, but we lucked up today, honey! I'm about to come scoop you up so we can go ahead and get in line. You know it's going to be long as fuck."

That was the best news Aianna had heard all week. She followed Slutty Vegan on Instagram but hadn't seen any posts about them coming to Houston. It was a dream come true. She jumped out of bed and ran to the bathroom.

She had to get herself together. She couldn't be in line looking a mess; every time she said she didn't care about her appearance, she ran into someone she knew. She wanted to be on her A game today.

⸎

"My eyes must be playing tricks on me. Tell me that's not Jess," Aianna said with her mouth gaped open. She and Terrance had been waiting in line for about ten minutes when she spotted her.

"Where?" Terrance looked to where Aianna was pointing. "Oh, shit! That *is* her! Who is that cutie she's talking to? I've never seen her before. Are you going to go speak?"

Aianna wiped her hands on her skirt. Her palms were sweaty all of a sudden. She and Jess had been lovers up until Jess moved to Chicago last April. They had communicated with one another for a few months, and then Aianna lost interest. Jess was cool, but Aianna wasn't used to having a long-distance "bae." If they had been in an actual relationship and not just fuck buddies, Aianna wouldn't have minded catching a few flights to see her instead of breaking it off.

"I'm not sure who that is. She's cute but too masculine to be someone Jess is fucking. And of course, I'm going to go talk to her," Aianna said sheepishly.

"Yeah, your ass wants to be nosy and see how long she's going to be here."

"You damn right! Jess's head game was something serious. If she's going to be here for a minute, I need some of that *tonight*!" Aianna laughed. "I'll be right back."

"I half want to be nosy and go with you, but I don't want anybody to say we're cutting, so I'll wait to get the tea when you come back."

There were about ten people in line between them and Jess. Aianna pulled out her hand mirror to make sure her lips were still glossy. She was glad she looked presentable, because Jess looked damn good. She had her fro pulled up into a pineapple and was wearing a crop top and some cargo shorts. The sun was hitting her cinnamon skin just right. Aianna popped a piece of gum in her mouth, strolled up to Jess and tapped her on the shoulder.

"Hey, Jess."

Jess was turned at an angle, so she had caught a glimpse of Aianna before Aianna noticed her. A six-foot-tall goddess, Aianna stood out wherever she went. Jess was going to go over and speak but wasn't sure how Aianna would react, so she had decided to wait. She was laughing at her silly roommate when Aianna tapped her on her shoulder. Jess turned around and acted like she was surprised to see her.

"Hey, love! How have you been? It's been a while."

"I've been good. Are you here for the weekend, or have you moved back?" Aianna wasted no time getting straight to the point.

"I moved back. Chicago was way too cold for me," Jess

replied, looking Aianna up and down. She was looking good enough to eat; Jess couldn't help but lick her lips.

Aianna caught Jess checking her out and smiled. "Cool. Are you free later? We should hang out if you're not busy."

"I'd love to catch up. Is your number still the same?" Jess was excited about *hanging* with Aianna. She knew exactly what Aianna meant when she said *hang*. The only time they'd hung out was when they were having sex. They had an undeniable sexual chemistry, but anything more than sex seemed to lead to unnecessary arguments.

"Yeah, my number is still the same. Hit me up later. I'm about to go back to my place in line. Everybody is looking at me like I'm cutting. I'm not cutting!" Aianna yelled out as she turned and strutted back to Terrance. A few of the bystanders chuckled, and a couple of others rolled their eyes. They weren't the least bit worried about her.

"So, what'd she say?" Terrance asked as soon as Aianna made it back to him.

"That she'll be free later to hang out with me. You know what that means? I'm getting my pussy ate!" Aianna laughed.

"Girl! You silly. I'm not about to play with you. It probably made her day seeing you, though. I'm ready for my day to be made by getting full. This line is long, and I'm so damn hungry my stomach is touching my back."

After waiting in line for close to two hours, they finally got their burgers. It was too crowded to sit inside and eat, so they headed back to the car.

"Aianna!" Jess called out to her. She jogged toward them, and they stopped walking to let her catch up. "Hey, do you want to ride back to my place with me? Tee's girlfriend came up here and scooped her up, so we'll have some alone time to catch up."

"Are you cool if I ditch you?" she asked Terrance, knowing he would be fine. He'd leave her in a heartbeat if some trade had come through for him.

"Do yo' thang. I'm about to go home, get full and go to sleep. Call me tomorrow, babe. See ya later." Aianna and Terrance exchanged hugs as he left.

"I'm parked in a parking garage a few blocks over. I hate paying for parking, but by the time we made it, all the curbside spots were gone. I'm really glad you saw me in line," Jess said. "I wanted to call you when I moved back, but since we hadn't talked in a minute, I decided against it."

Aianna shrugged. "You could have hit me up. I'm still single."

Jess changed the subject. "Is this your first time having one of these burgers? I got the Sloppy Toppy. I've heard good things about it, so I decided to see what the hype is about."

"Yes, it's my first time. I tried to go when T and I went to Atlanta, but we didn't get there on time. I got the One Night Stand, and I'm hype as fuck about it."

When they made it to Jess's car, she opened the passenger door for Aianna. Aianna hopped in and tore into her burger. "Oh, my God! This burger is fucking delicious!" Aianna said with a full mouth.

"I see. You damn near inhaled it!"

"Girl, I've been waiting to try this burger for hours, so I had to go ahead and dig in. Are you going to eat yours, or just watch me?" Aianna waved a fry in front of Jess's face while she talked. Jess leaned forward and bit half of it. Aianna seductively put the other half in her own mouth.

"I'm digging watching you right now. I'm not sure how you make eating look sexy, but somehow you do. I miss your lips; are they still soft?"

Aianna put her food on the dash and then did the same with Jess's food.

"I mean, you can easily find out. We're in an empty parking garage, and even if it wasn't empty, who's going to stop us?" She got out of her seat and hopped on top of Jess. Jess laid her seat back as far as it would go. Aianna leaned forward, put her hands on Jess's shoulders and started kissing on her cheeks. She stopped with a kiss on the lips.

"Hmm, I think they are, but I need to kiss you again to be sure," Jess teased. She slid her tongue inside Aianna's mouth and kissed her like it was her last meal. "Damn... they are still soft."

Aianna smiled and sat up so she could pull her top off. "My titties are still soft, too." She wasn't wearing a bra, so her breasts cascaded from underneath her shirt like a waterfall. She leaned forward again and grabbed the top of Jess's puff. Aianna's breasts swayed from side to side, which Jess took as an invitation to kiss and caress them.

"Hmm. So that's all you gonna do?" Aianna asked, almost in a growl.

Jess wanted Aianna in her bed, but since Aianna was asking for more, she delivered. Jess eased her hand up under Aianna's skirt and yanked her panties to the side. Rubbing her thumb against Aianna's clit a few times, Jess slowly inserted it inside her pussy. Aianna gripped Jess's shoulders, bouncing up and down on her thumb. The sides of their faces were pressed together, and Aianna was moaning in her ear. Jess was all the way turned on now. She pulled her soaking wet thumb out of Aianna's pussy. "Damn, I need to taste you. Now. Let's climb in the back seat, so we have more room."

Aianna pulled her panties off and threw them at Jess before she climbed into the back seat. Jess caught them, sniffed them and then tossed them onto the dashboard. Now Jess was more than anxious to eat her pussy. She pulled the driver's seat up as far as it would go and then climbed into the back seat. There wasn't much room to maneuver, but she could make it work. She squeezed Aianna's thighs as she dived into her pussy. Damn! If spring had a taste, Aianna's pussy would definitely be spring flavored. She continued to lick her juicy center while Aianna tugged on her puff. They were startled and jumped when they heard loud taps on the window.

"Oh, shit! It's security!"

TRISTA & LAUREN

H_2O

Trista and her wife, Lauren, walked into the ballroom arm in arm, both wearing black tuxedos. She wore a diamond pendant with Lauren's initials on her lapel. Her salt and pepper locs were in a tight bun, and Lauren's auburn hair was freshly faded. They had both picked up weight throughout the years, but they were still a beautiful couple. Trista was sure they were getting some stares, because that seemed to happen whenever they were out. *Let them stare* is what she had been telling Lauren for years.

She was annoyed that in 2019, most lesbians felt as if stud on stud was still taboo. It was mostly Black lesbians that gave them the looks of disapproval, too. To say love is love but then turn around and give studs flack about loving one another—what a bunch of hypocrites! Regardless of how they dressed, they were still women. Trista instantly became annoyed when people said it was weird or told them they must want to be gay men. What ran her hot was when people asked who the man was in their relationship.

It was stupid to her because she wasn't about to conform to heterosexual norms. Trista had always been attracted to masculine women and didn't feel ashamed about it. Lauren had recently deleted her Facebook account because she was tired of all the negative comments people were putting under their pictures. She had thick skin when it came to people insulting their relationship, but after years of being cyberbullied, she was over it with social media.

The couple had met when they were sophomores in college. Before she and Lauren became an item, Trista had spent most of her free time in the library. Her parents were constantly on her about making sure her GPA was exceptional, so she didn't want fun to interfere with her success. The night she hooked up with Lauren, some friends had convinced her to go to a Halloween party. Trista groaned but decided to go ahead and loosen up. She hadn't had any real fun since she started college. She knew one night wouldn't send her on a downhill spiral of irresponsibility. Trista had planned to go to the party wearing jeans and a t-shirt, but her friend, Nicki, wasn't having it.

"Stop being so boring. I'm dressing up as Beetlejuice. Let's go to the store and find you some kind of costume."

Trista felt overwhelmed as soon as they stepped inside the costume store. There were costumes, props and wigs everywhere. "Nicki, why the hell did you bring me to this damn store? I'll never be able to find shit in here," Trista had exclaimed.

Nicki shrugged her shoulders and scratched her head.

"I guess I didn't think too much about it being a wreck the day before Halloween. I'll help you find something. You want to be sexy or ghoulish?" she asked, holding up a Catwoman suit.

"You know damn well I'm not trying to dress sexy," Trista replied sternly.

After about ten minutes of rummaging through costumes, Trista found a braided wig and waved it around. "I know who I want to be. I'm Rick James, bitch!" They both laughed. That night would be Trista's first time ever dressing up for Halloween. Even though it was out of the norm for her, she was starting to get excited. She spent another five minutes looking for some red boots.

Nicki teased Trista when she saw her trying them on. "So, you know Rick James basically wore a Catwoman suit with red boots, right?"

Trista laughed but didn't reply. Nicki had a point, but she figured if she was going to dress up, she might as well go all out with it. By the time they left the costume store, she was excited about attending the party.

The party was packed and almost everyone was dressed in costume. Trista was having a good time laughing, joking and dancing with her friends. They were all on their second or third drinks, but she was still on her first. Trista wasn't much of a drinker, so that would more than likely be her only one. She scanned the room to see if any of her classmates were at the party. She spotted Lauren and had to do a double take. Lauren was fine. They had English class together, and Lauren was always wearing baggy jeans, so Trista had never realized how shapely she was. Tonight, she was wearing a purple jacket over a white ruffled blouse and no bra. Trista knew exactly who she was dressed up as. She smiled at the fact they both came dressed as music icons. Trista wasn't sure if she should go speak to Lauren or not. They had made small talk in class, but that was it. Lauren had the prettiest hazel eyes Trista had ever seen. She had curly, auburn hair that she always had pulled back in a ponytail. Trista never flirted with her because she wasn't sure if Lauren was attracted to masculine women or not. She never saw Lauren with anyone, so she assumed she was at least single. Trista decided she could either continue making assumptions or she could move past casual conversation and express her interest. What's the worst that could happen?

"Purple rain, purple rain," she sang once she was in Lauren's earshot.

Lauren giggled. "Hey! I was hoping people would know I was Prince. I see I did a good job creating this costume. You're Rick James, right?" Lauren had a big smile on her face as she extended her arms for a hug.

Trista was nervous. They had never hugged before, only dapped each other up. She took it as a sign that Lauren might have some interest in her. Either that or she was just being friendly. Trista didn't want to act as awkward as she felt, so she walked into Lauren's open arms and hugged her back. She caught a whiff of Lauren's cologne as they embraced.

Damn, she smelled good. She couldn't even remember what Lauren had asked her.

"You look great," Trista whispered in Lauren's ear while they were still locked in their embrace. "You smell good, too. What kind of cologne is that?" They let go of each other and Lauren took a step back.

"It's called Euphoria, and thanks," Lauren replied with flushed cheeks. She wasn't used to receiving compliments from masculine women. Maybe Trista was only being nice.

"And, oh, yes. I am Rick James. I almost forgot you asked me that. It's kind of funny we both switched it up for the night."

Lauren did a spin. "Yeah, and we both look really pretty, too."

Trista was trying to ask Lauren about her day, but someone walked up to the DJ booth and he cranked the music up. She leaned in a little closer. "It's too loud to talk now. You want to go out on the patio?" Trista asked, trying not to scream in Lauren's ear.

"Sure. Let me go get another drink real quick."

Trista nodded and waited for Lauren to return. They walked out on the patio and saw a couple in one of the oversized chairs making out. Lauren's cheeks instantly turned red. Trista noticed that Lauren seemed uncomfortable.

"You want to go back inside?"

"No, I'm fine. I was caught off guard because I didn't see them there at first," Lauren said. The couple continued their make out session as if they were still by themselves.

"I could never be that bold," Lauren whispered. She continued to stare at the couple as if she had never seen anyone make out in public before.

Trista smiled. Now was her chance to make a move.

"So, if I were to try to kiss you out here, would you reject me?"

Lauren laughed nervously before asking, "Is that a rhetorical question?"

"I guess it depends on what your answer is," Trista said, trying to read Lauren's expression, but half of her face was hidden in the shadows. Trista decided to make a move and gave Lauren a quick kiss on the cheek. She felt like a middle schooler, but she had to build up enough nerve to kiss Lauren for real. Lauren's body language let her know it was good. Trista leaned forward until their lips were almost touching.

"So, can I kiss you for real this time?" she asked in a whisper.

Lauren nodded and smiled, deciding she would be the one to make a move this time. She placed her hands on Trista's waist and kissed her passionately. Trista's lips were so soft and inviting. She had never kissed another stud before, but she realized it was no different from kissing a fem. She let Trista's hands roam all over her body. Her pussy was wet within seconds. Lauren wanted to let Trista's hands do more than roam, but Trista stopped kissing her and pulled back. Without saying anything, she walked toward an oversized loveseat in a dark corner.

Trista sat down and motioned for Lauren to come sit on her lap. "I want your back facing me," she directed with a smug look on her face. Lauren obliged and sat down on Trista's lap. This was all new to her, so she was going with the flow. "Part your legs," Trista whispered in her ear. Lauren's heart was racing, and her pussy was tingling. Trista eased her right hand into the front of Lauren's spandex.

"Hmm, a shaved pussy. I like that," Trista said in a low moan, nibbling on Lauren's earlobe. Lauren moaned back and gripped Trista's legs while she was being fingered. Trista started off slow and then gradually sped up.

"Damn! It feels so good!" Lauren shouted. "You want to get more acquainted somewhere more exclusive? Like my bed?" She didn't want the night to end.

"Hell yeah! Let's go." Trista slid her hand into Lauren's and they left the party. They were inseparable from that night on.

CAMBRÉ
Next Lifetime

Brooke's hands felt like magic as she massaged shampoo through Cambré's locs. It felt like heaven. What she knew would be even more heavenly was Brooke touching other parts of her body. She knew the thoughts about her hairstylist of two years were wrong, but she couldn't help herself. They had hung out a couple of times, but for the most part, Cambré only saw Brooke once a month for loc maintenance. Even though they weren't around each other often, they would have conversations as if they had known each other for years. Cambré wasn't sure what it was about Brooke that had recently piqued her interest, but for the past four months, there had been a lot of sexual tension between them.

When Cambré had arrived at the shop today, she took a good look at Brooke. Brooke had gained some weight, and it seemed to have gone right to her breasts and thighs. Unlike the last time Cambré was there, Brooke's hair was cut into a mohawk today. She had never noticed the pair of lips tattooed on Brooke's neck. Cambré wondered if it was a new tat or if she just hadn't paid attention before. All she knew was that Brooke was looking like a four-course meal.

Brooke was single, but Cambré was in a relationship. Cambré cared for her girlfriend, but lately things had been off between them. She didn't know if she was subconsciously creating a rift between them because she wanted to sleep with Brooke, or if her girlfriend was indeed acting different. Whatever it was, she knew she and Brooke needed to stay platonic.

"You're awfully quiet today. Is everything okay?" Brooke asked while she was rinsing Cambré's hair.

"I'm good. I'm just a lil' hungry. I didn't eat before I came," Cambré replied, but she knew she didn't sound too convincing. Cambré also knew she couldn't tell Brooke how she had been feeling around her.

Brooke had been feeling the sexual tension but wasn't going to bring it up, either. She had never hung out with Cambré's girlfriend, but she knew she had one, so Brooke wasn't going to step out of the friend zone. She towel dried Cambré's hair and had her take a seat in her chair. Brooke pulled out her homemade loc butter and started palm rolling Cambré's locs. After a few minutes of silence, she decided to make conversation.

"I don't have any more clients after you. I can block off my schedule and we can go have brunch if you want to."

Cambré hesitated before replying. "Uh, yeah. We can go have brunch. I'm free for the rest of the day, too."

"Okay, cool. I'm about to go up front and tell April to block off the rest of my day. I'll be right back."

Brooke went up front, so Cambré pulled out her cell phone to text Racheal, her girlfriend: *Hey, babe. I'm going to brunch once Brooke is done with my hair. Are you still at the office? I can bring you something if you'd like.*

Cambré kept her phone out to see if the bubbles would appear. When they didn't, she knew that meant Racheal was busy with work. When Brooke came back around the corner, Cambré tried not to stare at her, but it wasn't an easy task. Brooke was wearing a low-cut top that highlighted her breasts. They bounced with each step she took.

"Okay. We're all set. I'm almost finished with your hair, so we can head out. Do you know where you want to go?"

"Anywhere that has mimosas. I could go for some pancakes, too," Cambré offered.

"Cool. I know the perfect spot that has both. You want to follow me or hop in my car?"

"I'll ride there with you."

When Brooke was finished with Cambré's hair, she turned Cambré's chair around so she could look in the mirror. "You got me looking good, as usual. Thanks," Cambré said with a smile. She paid Brooke for her services and waited for her to clean up her station. While Cambré was waiting, her phone dinged. She pulled it out of her pocket: *Hey, I'm good, love. I'm going to the mall with Amber in a bit and then we're going to grab a bite to eat. See you later.*

Brooke took Cambré to one of her favorite brunch spots.

They talked about everything except the tension building between them. The tension that seemed to intensify after Cambré had her second mimosa. Her eyes were getting glossy. "These mimosas are good, but I better slow down before I end up on the floor," Cambré joked with slightly slurred speech.

"Yeah, that's why I stopped at one," Brooke answered. "Well, that and the fact that I'm the designated driver. We'd both be in here slumped over."

Cambré placed her hands on top of Brooke's. Brooke quickly moved them and placed them in her lap.

"I'm so sorry. I shouldn't have done that," Cambré said sincerely.

"What are we doing, Cambré? There's something going on between us, but you have a girlfriend."

"I know, I know. But what if I'm not supposed to be with her? What if I'm supposed to be with you? Nah, don't pay attention to me. I'm a little tipsy…maybe we should go."

"Yeah, I think that's for the best," Brooke agreed.

After Cambré paid for their food and drinks, they walked to Brooke's car in awkward silence. The silence continued as they made the drive back to the salon. Brooke opened her mouth to say something but switched on the radio instead. Damn. Erykah Badu's "Next Lifetime" had to be playing while Cambré was debating if she and Brooke should act as if they didn't have more than friend feelings or ignore them since she had a girlfriend. It was fucking selfish of Cambré to even have the thoughts about Brooke she was having, but she couldn't help it. She didn't want to feel the way she felt, but she did. It's always easier from the outside looking in, but when you're on the front line, it's more complex.

"So, let's clear the elephant out of the room...well, car." Brooke broke the silence with a nervous laugh.

"I'm sorry. I've been in my head this whole time. I like you more than I should, and I want to act on it. I might need to find a new stylist," Cambré confessed.

"Finding a new stylist might be what's best. I feel something, too. When I first started doing your hair, that's all it was. Then we crossed over to hanging out. It's been fun getting to know you, but I'm wanting to act on it, too."

"Yeah, I'm going to go home and sober up. We'll talk more about it later?"

"Yeah, that's cool."

"Oh, shit! My car keys aren't in my pocket."

"Did you leave them in the restaurant?"

"I don't think so. Maybe I left them in the salon. It looks like everyone is gone. You have a key, don't you?"

"Yeah. It's on my keyring. Come on. Let's see if they're inside."

Cambré stood behind Brooke while she unlocked the door to the salon. The smell of her perfume seemed stronger and more enticing. Fuck it, she wasn't going to subdue herself any longer.

"Here they are," Brooke called out, picking the keys up off of her work station. She handed them to Cambré.

Cambré stuck the keys in her pocket and pulled Brooke in to kiss her on her lips.

Brooke wanted to pull back, but Cambré's lips were so soft and warm. They stopped kissing, and Brooke put her hand across her chest. She was hot and bothered. She stood looking at Cambré for a few seconds and then initiated another kiss. Cambré let her hands roam all over Brooke's body while they kissed each other. Brooke pulled out of Cambré's embrace and pulled her top off. Cambré watched her with her lips slightly parted. Brooke's full breasts looked like they needed to be squeezed and sucked on. Cambré unhooked her bra and watched them spill out of it. As soon as she started unbuttoning Brooke's pants, her phone started ringing. Cambré ignored her phone and continued undressing Brooke. She got on her knees so Brooke could put her hands on her shoulders while she leaned from one side to the other to remove her pants. Then, Cambré pulled Brooke's panties down. Brooke's clit looked like it was screaming to be licked. She parted her legs to give Cambré easier access. Cambré eased a finger inside of Brooke and then took it out and sucked it. She needed to do a taste test first, and she was pleased with the outcome. Just when she was about to rub her finger across Brooke's clit, Cambré's phone started ringing again. She ignored it for the second time, but then it rang again.

"Fuck! I should have put it on silent!" Cambré yelled angrily.

"Maybe you should answer it. It could be an emergency," Brooke reluctantly told her.

Cambré pulled her phone out of her back pocket. "Damn. It's Racheal. Sorry, but I have to take this. Hello?"

PAIGE

Rehab

“Thank you, Mother Nature, for sending a natural disaster through my life like a wrecking ball! The timing couldn't be worse, because of all the people I could be trapped with, my ex didn't even make the list. Yes, I have a list. It mostly consists of people I wouldn't mind being trapped in an elevator with. Rihanna is number one. Aside from being drop-dead gorgeous, she seems like she would be a lot of fun to be around. We could smoke a blunt, and I would ask her to sing a song or two. That would be a dream come true. Granted, I would never be anywhere near her, even if she was in Houston.

“Fuck!” Paige yelled. She rambled whenever she was frustrated. She had been unaware she lived in a flood zone until she woke up that morning to car alarms going off. When she looked out of her bedroom window, every vehicle in the parking lot was submerged under water. “Fuck!” she yelled again and continued to stare out the window, wishing she'd wake up from her nightmare. She really wanted to freak out, but what good would that do? On the bright side, she had picked an apartment on the second floor, so she didn't have to be evacuated right away. She was also thankful she still had electricity, even though there was no telling how long that would last. She wondered why Mayor Sylvester had urged Houston residents to stay put. Maybe he didn't want people to panic, or maybe it was too risky to leave by the time he made the announcement. Whatever the case, people that knew they lived in a flood zone probably should have left as soon as they could.

Paige went to the kitchen and grabbed a bottle of wine. It was early, but so what? She figured she might as well drink since she couldn't do anything else. Mari, her ex, was asleep in the living room. She wasn't going to bother waking Mari up to break the news to her. She would find out when she woke up and tried to leave. Mari was usually off somewhere being a ho, so Paige wasn't expecting her to come home the night before. They had broken up three weeks ago, but their lease didn't end for another six months, so they were stuck living together until then.

Paige wished she knew someone who could take over her portion of the lease, because six months was going to seem more like a year. There was nothing but tension between them. Whenever they were home at the same time, they moved around the apartment as if the other person didn't exist to avoid arguing over dead issues. Now, with the flooding, they wouldn't be able to escape one another. It's crazy how one day you can have so much love for a person and then the next, you feel nothing. Well, Paige still loved Mari, but she no longer trusted her. What's a relationship without trust?

Paige had first noticed a change in Mari about a month before they ended their relationship. Whenever Mari said good morning, it seemed empty and forced. Their good morning kisses turned into quick pecks on the cheek as she was heading out the door. They used to text each other often throughout the day, but Paige had noticed the messages started being one sided. If she didn't text Mari, she wouldn't talk to her until she got home from work, and even then, Mari didn't ever have much to say. Paige tried to talk to her about her concerns but Mari would blow her off and tell Paige she was tripping. After a week straight of Mari coming home late from work without any explanation, Paige decided to go through her cell phone. Mari had a password on it, but Paige knew the code. Up until that moment, they had completely respected each other's privacy. Paige was tired of trying to talk to Mari about their problems, though. She needed to find out what was going on. The last message Mari had received was from her coworker, Trini. Paige was livid when she saw the number of messages and phone calls they had exchanged. Trini had been only a work friend for as long as Paige could remember; now, they were all buddy-buddy. That's why Mari was acting different. She had started fucking someone else. She walked in while Paige was going through her phone and things got heated.

"Oh, so that's what we're doing now?" Mari demanded with her hands on her hips.

Paige tossed the phone back on the bed. She didn't care that Mari had caught her snooping. "Yeah! Since you act like you can't talk to me, I had to look through your phone and see why." She got up and got in Mari's face.

The look in her eyes made Mari uncomfortable. She wasn't about to let her dominate the conversation, though. Mari put a hand on Paige's chest and pushed her back. "Talk?! Paige, it took you months before you decided to talk to me. I was already broken by then."

Paige waved off what Mari said as if it wasn't important. "Man, fuck that! How long have you been fucking Trini?"

Mari rolled her eyes. "We've never fucked."

Paige sucked her teeth and started pacing. "I don't believe that. If you can't be honest with me, there's no way we can repair our relationship."

Mari let out a deep sigh. "Once again, we're not fucking!"

Paige had had enough. She pushed Mari so hard she almost fell.

Mari was shocked. Paige had never gotten so mad that she put her hands on Mari. They stared at each other for a few seconds more, and then Paige grabbed her keys and stormed out of the apartment without any more words. Mari didn't try to go after her. What was the point? Paige wasn't willing to listen.

Paige got in her car and slammed the door. "Fuck!" she yelled, banging her hands on the dashboard. She wasn't going anywhere, but she had to get out of that apartment. She was so hurt and angry and wanted to do more than just push Mari down. They had been through so much. She couldn't believe Mari was willing to risk everything they were trying to build to occasionally lay up with another woman. There was no recovery from this, and she wasn't willing to talk about it. Mari was calling her, but Paige kept declining her calls.

Paige sat in her car for three hours. When she walked back into her bedroom, Mari was sprawled out asleep. Normally, she would scoot Mari over and lie next to her with an arm draping over Mari's body. Tears welled up in Paige's eyes. She couldn't do that tonight; she didn't want to be in bed with Mari. She grabbed a blanket and a pillow from their closet and went to sleep on the couch. They never made up after that night.

"Paige," Mari called out, standing in front of the doorway. Paige was lying in bed with her hands over her face. She had downed the whole bottle of wine and was feeling the aftermath.

She pulled her hands down and rolled her eyes. "What?" She never initiated contact with Mari, and it annoyed her when Mari tried to talk to her.

"Never mind." Mari huffed and rolled her eyes before storming out of the room. She wished she hadn't come home last night. Paige's attitude was always unnerving. Mari was saddened at how things had turned out between them. It was her choice to leave the bedroom they shared to sleep on the couch. She didn't feel right climbing in bed next to Paige since they were no longer an item. That was Paige's choice, not hers. She still wanted a relationship with Paige, even though Paige was being a blockhead. She let out a deep sigh and hoped they wouldn't be trapped together much longer.

It had been two days since Harvey tore up Houston. Even though she was thankful they still had power, Paige was tired of watching TV. She decided she would get out of bed and organize her closet since she had nothing better to do. While rummaging through a box of her knickknacks, she knocked over a box that was full of Mari's things. The journal she'd bought Mari was amongst the items. She bent down, picked it up and started flipping through the pages.

> *7-12-17*
>
> *It's only been three weeks since I miscarried, but Paige is walking around as if nothing happened. I cry myself to sleep most nights, and she doesn't even notice. To be with someone yet still feel alone…It's heartbreaking.*

> *8-19-2017*
>
> *I don't care that Paige became insecure within our relationship. She wasn't there when I needed her the most, and Trini was. I wouldn't be alive today if it wasn't for Trini.*

> *I was thinking about taking my life, and she talked me out of it. She's been a great friend throughout this ordeal, but Paige saw something else and let jealousy get the best of her. I love her, but I'm not about to continue to plead my innocence to her.*

Paige closed the journal and tried to swallow the lump of regret she felt in her throat. She had been a fool and an asshole for no reason. She grieved the loss of their child too, but secretly, so she wouldn't upset Mari any further. She was so gone in her own sadness, she didn't even realize she had shut Mari out. Damn.

Paige really needed to apologize, but she wasn't sure if Mari would be willing to talk after the way Paige had always brushed her off. She could show Mari the journal, but she knew Mari would be upset she had invaded her privacy once again. Paige swallowed her pride and went into the living room. Mari was curled up on the couch watching *Martin*.

"Hey, um...Can we talk?" Paige asked, twiddling her fingers.

"Really? Now you want to talk to me?" Mari replied sharply, smacking her lips. "Some nerve you have. You always want everything done on your time. You're fucking selfish!"

"You're absolutely right. I've been a jerk. An asshole."

Mari didn't respond; she only nodded. She had so much she wanted to say, but she needed to give Paige a taste of her own medicine. She glared at her for a few seconds and then stared back at the TV screen.

Paige expected as much but refused to back down. "I'm so sorry. I know saying sorry isn't enough. I want to make it up to you. I haven't been here for you for a while now. Can we talk? Please?"

"Paige, we never talked about my miscarriage. I don't care if it happened four months ago, you never mourned the loss of our baby with me. I don't know how you felt because you wouldn't talk about it, but what I do know is that you let me cry alone. You said nothing, Paige! The woman I loved let me grieve alone. After a while, it was hard for me to go through the motions and act as if everything was okay, so I shut the fuck down. Trini noticed I was down and became a really good friend. She was there for me in my time of need, and you weren't. It's that simple. If you would have actually taken time out to read all the messages, you would have seen that she and I only had a platonic relationship. What pisses me off the most is that I hadn't seen any real emotion from you until you decided I was cheating. When I tried to talk to you rationally, you flipped the fuck out on me. You wouldn't let me explain, so I got tired and gave the fuck up. I shouldn't have to prove shit to you, anyway."

"Damn. I was so sad, hurt and even angry when you had the miscarriage. I was also selfish because I shut down and didn't comfort you or even let you know how I was feeling. I'm realizing now that I'm the one that stopped showing you affection. You only acted according to how you were being treated. I saw what I wanted to see in those text messages instead of what was actually there. I brought on my own insecurities and created this rift between us. I'm so sorry and, again, I know saying sorry doesn't erase my behavior these past few months, but from this day forward, I'll show you with my actions. I want to rebuild so we can repair our relationship…if you're willing to allow me to do that." Paige smiled. It was warm and genuine. Her eyes showed that she was truly sorry.

Mari was hurt and angry, but she also missed Paige badly. Mari was willing to give her another chance. She walked up to Paige and put her hands on Paige's face.

"I'm willing to push the reset button so we can move forward. I love you." Mari wrapped her arms around Paige's waist and kissed her cheeks. She had missed Paige so much. To be living in the same space but disconnected from each other had been torture. It was heartbreaking, and it was the reason she would spend many nights away from the apartment. She looked down at Paige and kissed her passionately.

"So, I don't know about you but, uh, I'm horny," Mari purred.

Paige smirked and then cuffed the bottom of Mari's ass. "I would love nothing more than to lay down with you," she whispered.

"Can I strap you?" Mari asked with a raised eyebrow. Paige had only allowed Mari to use their strap on her one time in the length of their relationship. She could do without getting dicked down, but she was willing to let Paige have her way.

"Yeah. I'll let you fuck me, but missionary only. You did the most last time, when I let you hit it from the back," Paige laughed.

Mari grabbed Paige's hand and led her into their bedroom. She gently pushed Paige down on the bed.

"Get undressed," Mari told Paige, rubbing her palms together like Birdman. "I'm about to strap up." She could barely contain her excitement as she skipped to the closet to retrieve Paige's strap.

Paige chuckled to herself and got undressed. She grabbed her phone so she could put on her mood music playlist of Ari Lennox songs. She couldn't even remember their last lovemaking session; it had been that long since she had laid her eyes upon Mari's thick body. Paige sighed thinking about how foolish she had been and shook her head. There was no need to dwell on the past. She decided to focus on Mari undressing as she slipped underneath the covers.

Mari's titties bounced up and down as she adjusted the strap. Paige bit her bottom lip and shifted her body. She was happy they made up but didn't want to show it too much. Why was she trying to mask how she felt? She realized she was never as vulnerable in the bedroom as she could be. She decided she wouldn't subdue her moans like she normally did. She was so lost in thought, she didn't realize Mari was standing at the edge of the bed until she yanked the covers off of her.

"Are you ready for me, mami, or are you drifting off to sleep?" Mari asked with a big smile on her face.

"I'm ready, baby."

Mari pulled Paige to the edge of the bed and slowly eased the dong inside of her. Paige clenched the sheets and tossed her head back.

"Look at me," Mari demanded in a stern yet sultry voice. They'd spent months avoiding eye contact, so Mari wanted nothing less than to gaze into Paige's deep brown eyes. She thrust forward and eagerly kissed Paige.

Paige grabbed Mari's braids. "I want you to fuck me like there's no tomorrow," she crooned, breathing heavily.

Mari squeezed the back of Paige's neck and eased in and out of her pussy. Paige moaned and gripped Mari's waist, staring longingly into Mari's eyes. Mari put her hands on Paige's waist and picked up her speed.

"Yes, baby, that feels so good!" Paige yelled out.

"You like that?" Mari yelled back and put one of Paige's legs over her shoulder. She was enjoying fucking her. Mari pulled the dong out and put her head between Paige's legs. Her mouth was immediately filled with Paige's juices. "Ooh, baby, you taste so damn good. It's been too long."

"It has, baby...I'm so, so sorry. I promise I'll never doubt you again." Paige sat up in bed and locked fingers with Mari. "I want you to sit your pussy on my face." Paige unclasped her fingers and inched back to the head of the bed.

Mari got on her knees and walked to the head of the

bed as well. Once she was hovered above Paige's mouth, she took a seat as if she was sitting on a throne. Paige drove her tongue hungrily, as deep as it would go inside Mari's pussy. Mari slowly gyrated back and forth. Paige continued to swirl her tongue around. Mari tried to hold off on releasing, but she couldn't sustain any longer. She threw her head back and let out a moan as her creamy juices filled Paige's mouth.

"Mmm. That was so good," Mari whispered as she was easing off of Paige's face.

Paige licked her lips and smiled. "Yes, it was." She kissed Mari on her forehead and nestled her head on Mari's breasts. They had completely forgotten about being trapped until the power shut off.

Thank you for reading *Lesbian Sex Chronicles: First Session*
If you enjoyed this book, please leave an online review.

Keep in touch with Toi McMullen

Website: www.toimcmullen.com

Instagram: @sex_novelist

Twitter: @sex_novelist